Strange Boy

Paul Magrs

Strange Boy

SIMON &
SCHUSTER

SIMON &
SCHUSTER

First published in Great Britain by Simon & Schuster UK Ltd, 2002
A Viacom company

Simon & Schuster UK Ltd
Africa House, 64-78 Kingsway, London WC2B 6AH

A CIP catalogue record for this book is available from the British Library

ISBN 0 689 83657 0

3 5 7 9 10 8 6 4 2

Printed and bound in Finland by WS Bookwell

For my mam – Joy Foster – with love

With thanks to –

Louise Foster, Mark Magrs, Gladys Johnston, Charles Foster,
Arthur Foster, Rini Foster, Michael Fox, Nicola Creegan,
Lynne Heritage, Christine Booth, Mrs Payne, Pete Courtie,
Jon and Antonia Rolfe, Steve Jackson, Alicia Stubbersfield,
Meg Davis, Sara Maitland, Amanda Reynolds, Reuben Lane,
Georgina Hammick, Maureen Duffy, Shena Mackay,
Patricia Duncker, Marina Mackay, Victor Sage, Lorna Sage,
Stephen Cole, Andrew Biswell, Patrick Gale, Stephen Hornby,
Jo Moses, David Shelley, Bridget O'Connor, Peter Straughan,
Tiffany Murray and Larry, Carol Ann Johnson, Julia Darling,
James Friel, Justin Somper, Margaret Hope, Penny Webber,
Jon Cook, Val Striker, and, of course, Jeremy Hoad.

– P.M.

We're running through the woods.

We're crashing through the dark water of the burn that runs through our town and we're shinning up and down the trees of this whole wilderness.

That's what I'm doing with my best mate, John. And today's the day I decide to tell him about my super powers. My magical powers. I reckon today's the day to do it. We're both pretty worn out and red in the face from running about and everything. It's the kind of day when you can come out and say just about anything. The first thing that comes into your head.

I'm ten and he's fourteen or something.

We're hanging off the twisted heavy branches of the trees, which are all tangled up above. The leaves are like a fantastic canopy over our heads and you can hardly see the sky now. Below us there's the big drop down to the burn, which smells all sickly sweet.

Do I tell him? Is this the time? You've got to be careful with these things.

This will be the first time I've gone public – with

anyone – about my super powers. John is the chosen one.
Usually I'd be nervous of a bigger boy like him, but
John's OK really. He lives three doors down from us in
Phoenix Court with his mam, Mrs Blunt. Their garden is
bigger than ours and they've done nothing with it, Mam
says. They've still got packing crates and tea chests lying
about in it, with grass growing through, even though it's
months since they arrived from Australia. They're not real
Australians though, they only lived there a while, and it
didn't work out. Their tans have faded and now John and
his mother look like they've never been anywhere else but
here.

John's mam is depressed and religious all the time.
One day you'll see her and she's got jet-black hair. Dyed,
and plastic-looking in the sunlight. They next day, she'll
have bleached it all white. My mam reckons she'll have it
all drop out, doing that. She doesn't think Maddy has any
sense at all. It's like, one day she's saying she's a Jehovah's
Witness and the next she'll be back on with being a
Catholic. That's what she's like. It all happens overnight.

Mrs Blunt is depressed, Mam says, because her
husband ran off with this younger woman and now he's
having a new baby with her. Maddy pretends like she

doesn't mind. She's knitting things in preparation, like bootees and hats. She knits too tight and too loose and the things come out funny-looking. All the women in my family knit like crazy, so I know what that stuff is supposed to look like.

These days, Maddy is also painting religious murals on the back of old rolls of wallpaper. She's got them stretched out on her worktable in her front room. That's what she's doing this afternoon, while me and John are hanging in the trees down the Burn. She hasn't even asked John when he's going to go back in.

It's spring and it's mild and damp. The light's coming through the leaves with all this spangling green.

John is OK to have as a friend because he's not like the boys at school. They're all loud and they go round spitting and playing just the usual kinds of games. The latest thing is mashing crisps and Mars Bars together in your mouth and gobbing them on to the backs of people's coats. That's what they're like. But John's not.

'Growing up alone with a mother like that,' my mam says. 'No wonder he's soft. He's like a daft lad.'

What most people round the houses think is that John is weird. He's dark and tall and he looks just as depressed as his mother. He reads weird horror and fantasy comics. I've been going round quite a lot just lately, to read his collection secretly, because my mam thinks they give me nightmares. (Which they do, but then, I quite like having nightmares.) I think John and his mam quite like having the company.

In his bedroom John has the most fantastic posters: *Frankenstein*, *The Wicker Man* and Damien from *The Omen*. Most of these films I've never seen, so he explains to me what goes on in them.

He's four years older than me and already he seems like a grown-up man. He's got all these thick black hairs on his legs and under his arms.

One thing we've got in common: both our dads have walked out and left our mams alone in their square, black houses in Phoenix Court. John's mam knits and paints and does religion. Mine is seeing this new bloke who works at the electronics factory and might move in some day soon. Mam has the single of Paul McCartney's 'Mull of Kintyre' and she plays it all the time, again and again, as she makes up her mind whether to let Brian move in. Dad took nearly all of the records with him, as well as the furniture.

Sometimes it's best just to go playing out.

What really surprises me about John is that he listens to me like we're the same age. I can't get over that. And I end up saying all kinds of stuff, especially on the afternoons when we're hanging off the trees in the woods.

So I tell him.

At first he just stares at me.

His mouth is hanging open, but his legs are dangling and rocking faster in mid-air. You can tell he's really excited at the idea of me having the super powers. He's got all this dark stubble on his chin and lips. His hair's ruffled up, like he's just got up out of bed and come straight out to play. It's the summer holidays, so he probably has.

'No one has super powers really,' he says. 'That's just in comics.'

'I can read minds, transform objects into anything I want and sometimes I can make people say and do what I want them to do. Honestly, man, it's real.'

He blinks at me.

'I can pass straight through solid objects if I want. Walls and that. Intangibility, that's called.'

'Nah.' He shakes his head.

I shrug. I shrug as if to say: If you can't keep an open mind – you of all people – then I'm not going to tell you any more.

'It's true,' I tell him. 'Ever since I was a little kid. I've been able to do magic.'

'Hey, that would be great though, wouldn't it?' he says, like it's still a game or something. 'If it was true. I know the kinds of things I would do.'

'Well,' I say. 'I can.'

'Can you turn invisible?'

'Course.'

'If I could turn invisible, I'd go all over the place and find things out about other people. All their secrets. See what they get up to.'

'I do,' I say. 'I find out all kinds of stuff.'

He still looks sceptical. 'So how did you get these super powers?'

In the comics, this is what they call your Origin Story. Usually people have been attacked by a radioactive animal, like a spider or a leopard. Well, there's nothing like that in Newton Aycliffe, so I can't say that.

'I've always had them,' I say. 'As long as I can remember.

But you have to harness them and use them wisely, for the good of all mankind and that.'

'Course,' he says.

'Well, I first knew about them when I was about five, when I was kidnapped by a gang of evil older kids, and they locked me in a shed in their den on the waste-ground. I was all bound and gagged and they lit a big fire and danced around. I got out of that pretty easy.'

His dark eyebrows have gone up, surprised.

'My dad was looking for me all day. He thought I'd been, like, murdered. He got all of his policeman friends out to help him. But I freed myself and found my way home.'

'That's amazing,' he says. 'Go on, then. Show me. Show me something.'

I pause for a bit. In the gap of quiet we listen to all the rustling and creaking of branches, and the filthy gurgle of the burn below.

'It's not as easy as that,' I say.

'Why?'

'It's the kind of magic that's invisible to most people. It's not like wizards and witches, with flashes of light and thunderclaps and everything. It's very quiet. You have to be in the same world as me to be able to see it.'

He's frowning, and getting himself into a more comfortable crouch on the thick branch opposite me. The wood is all green with mildew and moss.

'You're in a different world to everyone else?'

'Course,' I say. 'We all are, really.'

'Bloody hell,' he says. 'I always knew there was something funny going on.'

'We're all in different worlds, so we can't quite see or know what other people are doing or thinking.'

'So can't you show me your powers?'

I look at John and make a decision.

'What I can do…' I'm talking slowly, more quietly – 'is pass you on just a bit of my powers. It might work. It might not. But with just a bit of my super powers, you'll be able to see what I can do…'

'Yes!' he says, too loudly, and I have to shush him. 'Yes, I'll do it!'

'Well,' I say, 'it's tricky. Like a ritual…'

'What do we do?'

We have to clamber down from our trees and go back to the den we've made on the ground. It's a kind of nest of dead branches and grass, all hidden among the trees.

We've got an old busted settee and a carpet. John's brought a rug and a tartan blanket from home. It's a great camp. It's the best one we've ever made.

We go crouching into it. The only thing about it is you can't stand up straight in there.

'This is how you pass the powers on,' I tell him. 'I don't know how I know. I've only done it a couple of times before…'

'Just tell me,' he says eagerly.

'It's how you let someone else into your world,' I explain.

'OK, OK,' he says. 'What do we do?'

His face is gleaming with anticipation. Now I'm going to have to tell him exactly what to do. He's four years older than me, but he really wants me to tell him. I can't believe it. Suddenly it's like he'll do anything.

'You have to take off all your clothes,' I tell him. 'Clothes get in the way of this.'

'Right,' he says, and starts tugging off his checked shirt. He wrenches it over his head and I'm surprised again, seeing the dark hair that's starting to show on his body, on all that pale skin. He pulls off his trainers, socks, and then he takes down his jeans.

'No one will see,' I tell him.

'OK.' He strips himself bare.

I'm taking a good look at his dick. It's a bit stiff and nearly as big as Simon's at school. Simon is the biggest lad in the class and he parades his dick around in the swimming-bath changing rooms. He can hang a wet towel off it and walk around. I think Simon is some kind of mutant freak. But John's is dead big too.

He stands there, waiting.

'Do you take yours off as well?' he asks.

'Yeah.'

I undress so he can't see mine. I hate to let anyone see mine.

Then, when we're both ready, I tell him that we have to lie on the leaves and under the blanket together.

'Are you sure?'

'Yeah. This is how we get into the same world.'

'OK.'

We lie down in the crackling, dead leaves. They smell musty and earthy. Somewhere there's a smell like petrol. We're going to be filthy with mud, I reckon. The twigs and stuff are sharp on us.

We pull the blanket over and lie face to face.

My heart's beating really hard and I can't believe what we're doing. His breath is really close and it's fast too.

Our clothes are hanging on the branches around us, hanging there like birds of prey, like pterodactyls with their wings all folded.

'Is it working?' John asks.

'All we've got to do is touch each other's dicks. You don't have to do anything with it. Just touch lightly at first, and hold on.'

'OK,' he says.

'Then we've got to close our eyes and concentrate.'

'Right,' he says, and we feel across to each other.

We lie like this for a while, our hands all hot. We're listening to planes going over and the birds singing – curlews, wood pigeons, cuckoos. The crackling of the burn.

'Is it working now?' he says. 'I think it is. I think I can feel it working.'

And so we lie like that for a while, hardly moving.

A bit later on, we're grabbing our clothes off the branches where we hung them and we get dressed quickly, picking twigs out of T-shirts and socks.

'I think I do feel different,' he says, tucking his shirt in.

'It'll take a while to settle in,' I tell him.

Then we run through the trees again, out of cover, away from the burn.

We run up the grassy hill to the houses. The back of John's house faces the woods and we bang on the window so his mam will let us in the back door.

John's mam is covered in acrylic paint and she's chewing a brush. She's dressed in black, like an old-fashioned widow. She's got a splash of purple in her wild, white hair.

'I suppose you've come to feed your faces,' she says. 'After all your running about like mad things.'

She sighs heavily and takes off her painting apron. She slips on her mules and goes off to the kitchen to make coffee. 'I've got some Battenburg cake for you boys, if you want.'

I'm looking at the mass of paints and brushes and jars of dirty, coloured water all over her worktable. She's let the whole thing take over her living room. My mam would never let that happen. Our front room is always spotlessly neat. Mrs Blunt has let her place go to hell. She must be concentrating instead on getting her art right.

She's watching me through the serving hatch as she waits for the kettle to boil. I'm staring at her new painting, which is just about as tall as John is. It's rolling up at the edges and the other side is all patterned and embossed.

The painting is of a sexy woman with her top half bare. She's opening her mouth to say something and her hair is hanging down in soft tendrils. And she's holding out her boobs. There's animals gathered all around her. A pretty weird selection of animals, I reckon. A cheetah, an alligator and a baboon. In the background there's an elephant.

John's mam has been borrowing my *Encyclopaedia of Natural History*. It's open at the elephant page on her worktable. She really likes the photos in that book. I reckon she's putting the animals into her painting just to show off. She's better at doing animals than she is people. The alligator is pretty good. It looks like it's going to bite the topless woman at any second.

'It's Mary Magdalene,' she says, though the serving hatch. 'You know, the woman Christ was in love with and would have married, if he'd got the chance? It's a portrait of her for the new Father. I'm hoping I can get it finished tonight, so it'll be dry in the morning when I go round to clean the church. I can roll it up and pop it through his front door without disturbing him. That's the beauty of painting on wallpaper. It rolls up beautifully.'

She brings us coffee in smoked-glass cups and saucers and a dinner plate of sliced Battenburg cake. We sit on the three-piece among her mess.

She seems to have gone gloomy again. 'But the painting isn't right,' she says. 'I think I went too mad on the animals. Too many, probably.'

'No, Mrs Blunt,' I say. 'I think they're great.'

She beams at me and says, 'Call me Maddy. We're not formal round here.'

John is over in the armchair, with his long legs stretched out in front of him. He's flicking through my encyclopaedia of animals.

'You're quiet,' his mam tells him.

He doesn't say anything. Sometimes I can't believe how rude he is to his mam.

'Have you had a good play out?' she asks me.

John looks up. His eyes look even darker and smudgier than usual. They're blazing. He nods at her.

'Yeah,' he says. 'Actually, we've got something to tell you, Mam.'

'Oh, yes?' Maddy brightens at this. It's like she wants to hear something out of the ordinary. She sits patiently, ready for John to go on.

'David and me,' he says, 'we've got a secret.'

She smiles at us both. 'Really?'

'Yeah,' he says, and looks at me.

I'm trying to communicate with him telepathically: No, don't. Don't spoil it. Don't tell her anything. She's not ready for it.

'Yeah,' he goes on. 'We've got, like, super powers. Like magical powers. We've both just discovered them. We're both super-powered, Mam.'

'Well!' says Maddy. 'Well, that's incredible!'

'It's true,' he says. 'We aren't really meant to tell you. But it's important. I have to let you know. Just in case anything happens.'

Maddy nods seriously. 'I'm glad you've told me. Powers like that can be a big responsibility, you know.' She looks at us both.

Well, I'm amazed at her. If I told anyone in my family about the powers, they'd laugh at me. I'd be laughed right out of the house. Maddy is just clutching her big knees and nodding slowly and looking very thoughtful.

Then she says, 'I bet you get these powers off me, John. I have a few magic powers of my own, you know.'

John's eyes go wide. 'You?'

Maddy smiles. 'Of course. Mental powers, things like that. Of course, I can't really go into it all now…'

John looks really flabbergasted.

Maddy passes us both another slice of the pink and yellow cake. I don't like the marzipan much, but I take a bit, just to be polite.

'Mind,' she says, 'you two boys, you have to be very careful. You have to watch out how you use these magic powers of yours.'

'Yes,' I say solemnly.

'And you must only ever use them for the good of humanity and all mankind.'

We nod at her.

John still looks amazed at what his mam is telling us.

'I presume you can both fly?' Maddy says, picking up the last sticky crumbs of her cake with the end of her finger. 'And read minds and turn invisible and all that?'

John and I stare at each other. We nod.

'Thought so.' She takes a big swig of her coffee, leaving just the molten sugar in the bottom of the glass cup. 'I was about your age, David, when I found that out about myself. I thought our John was a bit late in developing. I didn't think he was going to have any kind of powers at all.'

We both look at John.

'David helped to bring them out,' he says.

'Good.' Maddy smiles. 'Well done, David. Now, if you've both finished your coffee, I'd better chase you out. I've got to get on with the rest of Mary Magdalene's elephant.'

John shows me out of their house.

In the kitchen doorway he stops and he's staring at me.

He says, 'You made her say all that, didn't you? You were using your powers to control my mam's mind, weren't you?'

'No!' I say. 'She said it all by herself.' But then I'm thinking, maybe I did. Maybe I was taking control over her mind just then, without even knowing it. Sometimes powers like these can get scary.

John shakes his head, looking confused. 'OK. But don't you tell anyone what we did,' he warns.

'They're secret powers.' I shrug. 'Course I won't.'

'And I didn't touch you,' he says. 'You never touched me.'

'All right,' I say.

Then we say goodbye and I fly down the street to our house.

But we have touched each other, I'm thinking. Whatever he says now, we did do all of that. I can still feel all the prickly grass and leaves and stuff on my back and legs.

I can still feel the heat of his breath. And the blood is still whizzing round inside me. It's too fast, too hard to be normal.

2

My parents had me very young. They were just about kids themselves.

They decided to keep me and to get married and, when I found that out, I was pretty glad they did.

Not so much the getting married bit. I mean the bit about keeping me.

They got married in the summer and my mam's family didn't turn up because they didn't approve, but my dad's side did.

It was with them that my mam – and then me – ended up living.

I was due at the end of that year. They moved in with my dad's parents and they had a small bedroom at the back of the house, where the railway lines ran through the night.

This was in South Shields, ten years ago. It's right on the seaside, 30 miles north of the New Town where we live now. South Shields is an old town and, to hear the family talk, it's the centre of the universe. Newton Aycliffe is just a dump; a shopping precinct, factories, miles of black mud and council houses. That's where we are now.

Sometimes I think it's my super powers that let me remember everything that's ever happened to me, and everywhere we've lived. I've got memories going back to my first day on Earth.

Even better, I know what went on before I was born.

Maybe that's because my mam has told me all of it, like a fairy tale.

Or maybe my super powers do let me see into the past.

My mam was very young. She was just 16 and the move to this other family was a bit of a shock to her. She was pale and thin and she would try to sit to one side, out of the way, when her new husband's family were all together. They were noisy and she wasn't used to that.

If I concentrate really hard, I can see them all sat around. Clearly, like watching them on telly.

My mam would try to sit so that no one would notice her.

She had no choice about being there. Her own mam had thrown her out for getting pregnant. She just had to make the best of being with this new family.

My dad's family were raucous and loud. They shouted and drank and smoked and swore. They shouted out
loud at the telly when the football was on. They ate their
supper off trays on their laps in the front room. They ate
sausages and chops and mince, and everything with chips
and baked beans. They got the meat cheap because my
Little Nanna and Granda ran a butcher's shop on the
main street in town.

The one who ruled the roost round their house was,
of course, my dad's mam, Eileen. She was about to
become my Little Nanna – and she was, in fact, quite
little. But she was noisy.

She rattled and jangled with all sorts of jewellery,
including a charm bracelet my Granda had once bought
her, and to which she had been adding charms for years.
She once showed me a tiny box of glass with a five-pound
note folded up inside. For emergencies, she said.

She wore a leopardskin coat, white plastic boots and
had a black wig that she kept attached to her head with
hair-clips. She sang on the stage in working men's clubs
all over South Shields, doing her dramatic Shirley Bassey
impressions. She also captained several ladies' darts

teams. No night out in those days was complete without my Little Nanna getting up on the stage and giving her 'Goldfinger.' She would fling out her arms and whirl herself about under the lights.

Her husband was quiet and bald and a butcher. He would do anything for her. He was devoted to her, my mam's always said. Around the house he was like a slave: mopping the kitchen floor, hoovering around everyone in the front room. He would even lift up my Little Nanna's legs for her as she sat in her golden armchair, and hoover underneath her while she carried on singing or telling whatever story she was on with.

They had two daughters and one son and, with my parents' marriage, all of them were fixed up and settled by 1969. Weekends round their pebble-dashed council house in South Shields were crowded, smoky and loud.

My mam could hardly believe the way they carried on. They had a white leatherette bar in the corner of their front room. When the telly wasn't on full blast, they'd have a cocktail music LP on the stereo, or a *Themes from the Great Movies* record playing, and they'd be whizzing up cocktails and spirits and the soda siphon would be whooshing away and everyone would have to have a drink. Everyone had to be in the swing of things.

Early in November of that year the place was festooned in fairy lights already. My Little Nanna could barely restrain herself from getting that Christmas tree up and decorated. It always stood by her armchair, at the centre of attention. It was usually draped in so much golden tinsel and had so many glass baubles hanging off it that it didn't even look like a tree any more. This year, my Little Nanna was anxious for Christmas to come early.

My mam knew this was down to her.

That year, her whole life had changed around completely.

She had met Tom and they had started going out, even though he was a couple of years older than her and her mam wasn't keen on the whole business.

But my mam's mam (who was about to become my Big Nanna) couldn't keep her under lock and key for 24 hours a day. This was the 1960s. There were a lot of places to go out to, even in a small, old, seaside town like South Shields. It might not have been the bright lights of the big city, but there was still fun to be had. Mam's older sister and her twin were always out. They were out till all hours. My mam just wanted to be a part of that.

She had always been the quietest one. She'd been ill at 13 and hadn't been able to leave the house much then. She felt that she had some catching up to do.

It was the end of the 1960s too, and there was so much going on. Everything was changing. The whole world was going to be different.

And anyway, she had been convinced that you couldn't get pregnant the first time. She didn't think it happened like that.

But you could, it turned out, and it did.

And here was I, about to prove that stuff like that could happen.

Mam always used to be thin and pale. Elegant. Suddenly she had this bump. But you can't see it on the wedding photo, where she's in a white minidress with her dark hair hanging down. She's clutching Dad's arm and they're both surrounded by his family. All the women are in minidresses, floppy hats, dangling their handbags, and their eyes are made up with sky-blue eyeshadow. All the blokes look like gangsters.

The whole, small wedding group is posing in a back

alley in South Shields, standing by Dad's newly bought Hillman Triumph. He's holding his car keys carefully as my mam grasps his arm. She's wondering where her own mam and sisters are. Surely they could have come out and seen her get married?

Together, standing by that car, my mam and dad look as if they're going to make a fast getaway.

Dad had just joined the police force. That's what he was going to do to support the new family. Become a policeman.

It would take them a little while to get a house of their own. A year or so, when Dad came off his basic training. In the meantime, they would live with my Little Nanna and Granda. And then, of course, me.

I was born at one in the morning, as a storm went on, raging outside, whipping the sea up to crash on the cliffs of Marsden Bay.

My mam was left alone, after the birth, with me. They had dressed me in a brushed-cotton nightie.

She slept a little while, exhausted, and woke to have her very first, clear impression that she was not alone in that room. This was her first sense that there was another person present. One she was responsible for.

It had been a reasonably easy birth, she had been told. I hadn't come out all wrinkled and red.

Mam had been in labour all that evening without even really knowing it.

At tea time she had taken the bus across town to my Big Nanna's house, to try and make things up with her.

It was an escape for the afternoon from my dad's noisy family, and a relief to go back to her old home.

My Big Nanna was living with a devil of a man, her second husband, called Frank. Theirs was a curious marriage, with their own separate children, who weren't allowed to meet, and their food kept apart in the fridge. Their house was cold and stark, and filled with old furniture.

My mam ate tea at the kitchen table with her twin sister and her mother. It was the first time they'd really been together since she'd been thrown out. Bald, horrible Frank kept popping through, to keep an eye on them, and to check that they weren't eating anything that belonged to him.

My Big Nanna wasn't speaking to him that day. She wasn't speaking to him on most days. She barely said any-

thing to my mam, either. She laid out tinned-pork sandwiches and she poured out tea, into the best china cups,
treating Mam as if she were a visiting stranger.

My Big Nanna was tall and formidable, wearing a
high-necked jumper and a crocheted waistcoat. Her hair
was permed and dyed mahogany brown. Her lips were
tightly pursed, as if she was constantly holding back from
saying something that was on her mind.

That tea time, my mam was in pain, and kept rushing
to their downstairs toilet to throw up.

When Dad turned up in the liver-coloured car to pick
her up, he could see something was wrong. She was paler
than ever.

They hurried back to his parents' house in Chaucer
Avenue where, at the top of the stairs, on her way to their
bedroom for a lie-down, she was sick, again.

She didn't know what was happening to her.
It grew later and later. The pains were getting worse. I
knew what was going on.

The men fussed around her. My dad and his kindly
father with the sticky-out ears.

Meanwhile, my Little Nanna was giving a final,
farewell performance that night at a club. As the audience

sat with their pints and their Babycham, she filled the stage and gave it her all as Shirley Bassey.

Eventually, full of triumph, full of aplomb, and still singing, my Little Nanna returned home in full costume.

She never had time to describe all the details of the evening show, as she usually did. She saw the men's worried faces and went upstairs. After one look at my mam she took immediate charge. She told my dad to get my mam to hospital. This was it.

Mam was borne out into the street again, with sick still in her hair.

It was just about the 12th of November 1969.

They got her to the right place. The hospital was high up and facing the hectic sea. The nurses settled her in, with a room of her own. They told my dad he might as well go home and rest. There was going to be a wait.

Just as the storm took off in earnest, my mam listened to the noise of her husband, as he roared away in his Triumph. She could hear him leaving the car park, speeding off down the street.

And then, just like that, I was born.

Everybody missed it.

The nurses were down the corridor, having a cup of

tea and a fag. When they discovered they had missed the actual birth, they were scared they would get into trouble. One of them said to my mam, 'You'll not tell, will you? You never told us you were only 16. We'd have looked after you better if we'd known.'

Anyway, we slept.

It was a relief to be born. I had a good look around the place before I went to sleep.

In 1969 my dad's family never had a phone. My dad ran down the street at seven o'clock in the morning, to the phone box on the corner of Chaucer Avenue. He wasn't even fully dressed. He was in jeans, pyjama top, bare feet. After phoning the hospital and getting the news, he went running back up the street to their house, shouting.

That afternoon, his whole family came to see me.

There I was.

'Oh, isn't he big? He'll be a rugby player, a football player. An athlete. And look how bright his eyes are! He'll be a brainbox. He'll be a genius!'

For that family, only the best would do.

It took a few days before my Big Nanna came to visit us. She was working as a school dinner lady and couldn't get there any earlier, she said. My mam's twin sister didn't come to see us at all. My Big Nanna had put her off: 'We don't want to go drawing attention to it. We don't want to be making a big fuss.'

My Big Nanna also didn't want to be there when my dad's family were there. She thought they were a common lot and didn't want her daughter mixed up with them all. Though it was too late for that now. She certainly didn't want to see my dad's mam. They were both called Eileen, but they had absolutely nothing in common, apart from us.

My Big Nanna thought that my Little Nanna thought far too highly of herself. 'Singing like that bally Shirley Bassey. Who would want to do that? She doesn't even sing the words anyway. She just shouts. It's all to get attention to herself. And anyway, she isn't even black!'

When my Big Nanna turned up at the hospital in her headscarf and fawn camel hair coat, she sat on the opposite side of the bed to my crib and she wouldn't say much. Her face went red as she spoke to her daughter.

'You haven't got any make-up on, our Mary. You look terrible.'

Mam didn't care. She watched the way her mother's

eyes were fixed on the candlewick bedspread. 'Aren't you even going to look at him, then, Mam?'

My Big Nanna sniffed. 'I'm full of cold. He'll get my germs.'

But she leaned over to look.

I had white hair and blue eyes. And I looked straight at her.

'Eee! Well, he's bright as a button. And he doesn't look like anyone else in the family. Are you sure he's ours? Are you sure he hasn't just dropped from outer space?'

After my Big Nanna went, my mam picked me out of my cot and told me two things very clearly: 'You are going to be able to do exactly what you want to do, all your life. And you'll never have to do anything you don't want to. That's a promise.'

And I said to her, 'Fantastic!'

She almost dropped me in surprise.

3

When you walk into our house it's weird, because you go in through the kitchen and then into the dining room and that's the same room as the front room, because it all goes round in an L shape. They call it open plan.

These are new houses. We were the first ones to move into this house, when it still smelled of cold, damp plaster. The central heating comes out in warm gusty breezes from these ventilators near the floor.

'It's Ultra Modern,' my Little Nanna said, back when they used to come visiting. 'It's all Ultra Modern round here.'

All the grandparents came down together to look at where we were living. I can't believe that now, that they'd all get in the same car together to visit. You wouldn't catch them in the same town as each other now.

Ours was one of the first square black houses set up on the hill at the edge of the estate. There were acres of chewed up black and yellow mud all around us, and deep puddles of what looked like cold tea. All of the tractors and the digging machines were still lying about the place, ready to get on with building the rest of Phoenix Court.

My Big Nanna was singing a song about 'Little boxes... on a hillside.' because that's what our new estate looked like to her. We were living in Legoland, she said. Toytown.

When they moved in, Mam and Dad got straight on with decorating.

They had this whole new house to fill and to do up. They painted and papered and sanded down the banisters. I borrowed some of the sandpaper and started doing the doors to help out. Dad belted me because the doors were already varnished. Mam wouldn't talk to him for a fortnight after that.

They got this wallpaper for the front room that was all patterned with bricks, like orange-brick walls. Kind of old-fashioned. It's still up. It looks like the house is inside out.

We've got a three-piece suite that you can break up and move around and put in different positions. The corner bit is like a square coffee table that opens up and there's room inside for magazine and toys, stuff you're hiding. The dining table is brown smoked glass, and

when we're all at it having our dinner, you can see everyone's legs through it.

We eat off smoked-glass plates and we've got glass
cups and saucers too.

'Everything's see-through!' my Big Nanna laughed.

We've got this huge square window in the L-shaped
living room. Mam says it's the showpiece of the house.
It's a real feature. We've got a view through it of the
grassy hill down to the burn and all the trees. You can see
the hill on the other side, the one that our school's
behind. Woodham Burn Infants and Juniors. You can't
see them from here. You've got to go down this hill, over
the bridge and up round the other hill. It's the way Mam
walks to the town centre every day.

'You could almost be living in the country,' my Little
Nanna said.

When I get in, Mam's doing the tea in the kitchen. It's a
bit early.

There's a frying pan ready on the oven ring with fish
fingers in. They're frozen and whitish. A blob of lard sits
in the middle of them, waiting to get melted down. It's
not time to put them on yet.

Mam's hair is long and shining, newly washed and dried. She's got make-up on, her eyes are all dark, and she's wearing a long blue dress with little green flowers embroidered on.

When I come in she's reading the back of a bag of oven chips for the instructions. Oven chips are the new thing. We've watched the adverts and they reckon that there's no risk of chip-pan fires with them.

'Hey,' I go. 'Frozen food.'

We've not had frozen food since Dad took the fridge with him. We keep the milk bottles in a biscuit tin filled with cold water. It's like my Big Nanna says: 'What kind of man would take a fridge away from his bairns?'

'We have to eat them tonight, straight away,' mam says. 'Otherwise they'll go off.'

We've been having things from the bakery – pasties and pies and sausage rolls and that – since we haven't had a fridge. Mam has to go down the town every day to get the shopping in fresh. There's not a shop for miles around here. That's one of the drawbacks of living on this estate, she says. When we moved in, we had Dad and he had a car. That made it easier.

'Here, you'd better eat this now, as well,' she says.

It's a Bird's Eye mousse, and another one for my brother and two teaspoons. Now, these would definitely go off without a fridge. Though I quite like it when you lift the lid up and they've gone a bit runny. The jam stuff going through the fluffy mousse in spirals. Me and Christopher do this thing with raspberry-ripple mousses – you spoon everything out of the tub, into your mouth, and you're not allowed to swallow. The winner is the one who can get a whole mousse in their mouth at once. It's really hard to do. And Mam would go mad if she knew we did it sitting on the settee.

'Christopher's got his cartoons on,' she tells me. 'Don't you get mucked up. Brian's coming round to have tea with us tonight.'

'Why?'

She looks at me funny and then turns to give the frozen fish fingers a poke – which is pointless, because they're not switched on.

'I mean, why's he not having his at home with his Mam and Dad?'

She shrugs. 'I don't know. He's just having it here. With us.'

This sounds funny to me, but I don't say

anything else.

I'm going to have my mousse. We don't bother about things ruining your appetite round here.

Christopher's got *Playschool* on. He's six, so I suppose it's still the kind of thing he likes.

He sits on the settee, right back, and his legs don't even reach the edge. His hair is darker than mine and he's got this calf lick that makes it spring up at the front. His eyes are big and dark like Mam's and I suppose he looks more like her than I do. I'm supposed to look like my dad.

'Just so long as you don't take after him,' Mam always says.

'Aye,' my Big Nanna will add, if she's there. 'Don't take after that beggar.'

Christopher's got these dimples in his cheeks that everyone goes mad over and thinks are cute. He hates anyone mentioning them.

I sit with him on the settee and ask him what's going on.

He sighs. 'Big Ted and Little Ted and Jemima and Humpty and all that lot are supposed to be on a boat, sailing to America. But it's just a couple of cardboard boxes, really.'

We watch them for a bit, eating our Bird's Eye mousses. We don't do the whole-thing-in-your-mouth-at-once thing.

'That Brian's coming round for tea,' I tell him.

He looks at me like he has no idea what I'm talking about.

Mam comes through to see that we're behaving. She's walking fast and flicking her hair.

'Did you have a nice play out?'

'Yeah.' I turn round and tell her. 'It was great.'

Christopher looks along and gives me a nasty stare. He's not really allowed out of the front yard and he hates me for playing out.

'Did you go down that burn again?'

'No, Mam.'

'I've told you about that. You don't know what's down there.'

Then she sighs and remembers what she came through to the L-shaped lounge for. She hurries to the record player and switches it on. 'Mull of Kintyre'. As it starts, she's staring out of the feature window, straightening the slide in her hair, which is new, by the looks of it.

Brian comes round in a blue leather coat with loads of pockets and wide, flapping collars. He's in the jeans he wore for work at the electronics factory. He tells Mam that he never had time to change.

He's got this beard like a country and western singer and a yellow Ford Capri, which he's driven round to ours in, even though he lives with his parents on the other side of the estate.

We watch him when he comes in and talks with Mam. We watch to see if they kiss hello. We always listen to hear if he's got an Australian accent, but it's hard to tell because he's got a stammer. It's because of his stammer, Mam says, that he doesn't really talk much to us, only to her.

It's odd to think, now, that last summer Brian used to play tennis and all that with Dad. The lot of them used to be friends together – Mam and Dad with all the Australians. Brian and his sister would come round to play Monopoly. Dad took it too seriously and went mad if he thought they were cheating. Once he threw the whole board across the L- shaped lounge.

We heard the row from upstairs. Mam was laughing at him after the others had gone. She called him a big spoiled kid and he went crackers. He tore the dress off her back and took it out to his car with him and drove all the way to my Little Nanna's. I thought that was a weird thing to do, taking my mam's dress with him.

We watched him drive off that night, through the upstairs window. We didn't think he'd come back, but he did. Not for long, though.

'That was the beginning of the end, that,' Mam always says. 'That Monopoly night.'

Tonight Brian's brought a present for Mam. It's something he's made out of spare electronic components. He's supposed to be a wizard with electronics.

'Oh, look, you two,' Mam calls out, holding up this thing he's made. 'Look what Brian's given me.'

It's one of those games made out of bent wire coat hangers. You've got one of those little hooky things that you have to move around the wire shape, and if you touch the wire, it electrocutes you and sets the buzzer off.

'Isn't Brian clever?' she asks us.

We're hanging over the back of the settee to get a look at the thing. Brian's just standing there, looking pleased.

I'm thinking, it's the Etch-a-Sketch giraffe all over again. The first time Brian came round he got his hands on my Etch-a-Sketch and, after twiddling the knobs for about an hour, he drew this giraffe. We kept hearing about how brilliant it was, and I wasn't allowed to shake the Etch-a-Sketch and wipe it off. It had to stay on all that night.

Mam gives us a hard look. 'Don't hang over the back of the settee,' she says. 'It's not a slum.'

The wire thing has been bent in the shape of Basil Brush.

'Yeah,' I tell her. 'That's really good. It's in the shape of Basil Brush, isn't it?'

Mam looks at it again. 'Oh, God! It is!' She laughs, seeing the shape of the puppet fox in it for the first time. 'I never even saw it! I just thought it was a shape!'

How come Brian thinks Mam likes Basil Brush? How come he thinks she likes games? He mustn't have a clue.

He's brought a new record round, too. The Eagles.

He puts it on and Mam says they're his favourite. She likes them too now. Then she goes back to the kitchen to open a tin of peas.

When they're out on our smoked-glass plates with the oven chips and fish fingers and loads of tomato sauce, and when we sit down for our tea, I realise too late: they're processed peas. I can't eat them. Really, they taste like sick. I open my mouth to say something. Mam sees and flashes me a look. Don't you dare, in company. Just eat the buggers.

I leave them till last, though.

'If you eat them,' Mam says, 'I'll let you have first go on my Basil Brush coat-hanger game.'

'I don't want electrocuting.'

She laughs. 'It won't electrocute you! Brian's an expert at electronics!'

'You should have first go, anyway,' I say. 'He made it for you.'

She's gathering up our plates. 'Oh, I'd be hopeless at that. I couldn't hold that hook steady on the wire. Not with my nerves.'

Christopher's looking from Mam to Brian and he's smiling. It's like he's saying: 'There – that's a useless

present. You don't know anything about Mam's nerves.'
Or maybe he's just smiling.

That Basil Brush game looks to me like the kind of
thing that will end up chucked in the cupboard at the top
of the stairs. Never to be seen again. Or, like, years later,
someone will pull out this bit of twisted wire and say,
'What was this meant to have been?'

Mam says that's one good thing about these square
box houses we're living in. There's plenty of storage
space. So we've got this walk-in cupboard at the top of
the stairs. Christopher and I reckon there's probably a
magical land at the back of it. But you'd never get that
far, through all the heaps and piles of junk. Old coats,
clothes in bin bags, stuff of ours we've forgotten we had.
Loads of Dad's gear he still hasn't taken.

We sit along the settee to watch *Charlie's Angels*. It's all
that's on. It's a rubbish night for telly.

Mam brings cups of tea on a tray. Later on we'll have
crisps and chocolate. There's a set pattern to what we do
each night. Brian's fitting into it. He's sat next to Mam
with his arm along the back of the settee.

'Hey,' Mam says, out of the blue. 'Brian's on about

going to the pictures next week. Friday night. In Darlington. His Mam and Dad are going as well. Do you fancy it, you two?'

'What are they going to see?'

She looks at him. 'What was it again? Something daft.'

He's staring at the telly, over his mug of tea. *The Giant Spider Invasion,'* he tells Mam.

'That was it.'

Sometimes he doesn't stammer at all.

Christopher's looking really bored at *Charlie's Angels.* We never used to watch it. American rubbish, Mam would usually say. Brian and all his family love anything American. Mam says that's because they're Australians.

Brian's sister Kate and her husband and their two kids sold everything they owned in Wollongong and went on a cruise around the world, to Disneyland and Mexico, and then they came to England. After all that they came penniless to Newton Aycliffe, where the rest of the family had immigrated to. Their kids missed six months at school because they were in America, and that's why they can't read.

'Do you fancy it, then?' Mam asks. *'The Giant Spider?'*

Christopher says, 'Dad always takes us to the pictures on Saturday.' He comes out with it before I can stop him.

'Well,' Mam says, 'you can go two days running. That's a real treat. God, when I was a kid, I wish I'd had people offering to take me to the pictures every day.'

'We're going to see *The Wilderness Family*,' Christopher says. 'It's about a family who live at the North Pole with bears and that.'

Mam turns to Brian. 'He just takes them to see whatever's on the matinée. They've seen some rubbish with him. He keeps wanting them to play football or something and then he wouldn't have to think up what to do with them when he has them. But they won't do stuff like that.'

Brian nods.

I look at Mam. 'Are you going to go to this spider film, then?'

'Me? God, no,' she says. 'You know I can't go to the pictures. Not with my eyes. I'd get a migraine. No, I thought you could go with Brian by yourselves. Like big boys.'

When it's time for us to be getting our pyjamas on, Brian gets up to leave. Mam's telling him he needn't go yet, but he's pulling on his blue leather jacket. He's got to be at work in the morning.

'Thanks for the coat-hanger game,' Mam tells him. It's sitting on the dining table still. No one's plugged it in and had a go on it.

Mam gets us to say good night to him politely.

Then she's showing him out the back door, in the kitchen.

Round the corner, I can hear her saying to him, 'It was OK, wasn't it? Not too bad?'

They must be standing on the doorstep. By now, the street-lamps will be coming on, buzzing, pink then glaring yellow.

You can't pick out Brian's words. Just the low mumble of his voice.

'They're only little kids, really. They're good kids. They'd take to anyone,' Mam's saying. 'It'll just take time, that's all.'

We'd better go and get our pyjamas on. Otherwise Mam'll be thinking we're listening. The back door bangs, the venetian blinds rattle, and she's coming back into the front room alone.

'He left his Eagles record,' she says. She flops down

on the settee and looks tired all of a sudden. 'Are you two going to get ready for bed?'

I nod. 'Is he coming for tea tomorrow night, as well?'

Mam covers her eyes. 'Oh, I don't know.'

I tell her, 'We'd go to this giant spider thing... if you were coming as well.'

She lets her hands drop. 'You could have made more of an effort, you two. You're old enough now. You could have at least talked to him, you know. It wouldn't have hurt.'

'Why?' Christopher asks, standing in the middle of the rug, scuffing it with one bare foot. His sock is in his hands.

'Because I want him to feel at home here,' Mam says. 'I'd like us to be like a family.'

4

I've only been to the pictures at night once before. It was years ago.

It's funny going to the pictures at night because you come outside and it's dark. All the shops are shut, the lights are on, and there's stacks of people going about.

Dad took me to see *Jaws* one night when I was five.

He snuck me in to a film that was too old for me, probably because he was a copper. Mam says coppers think they can do what they want.

When we got home after the film, he was gabbling on to Mam about how great it was. 'It was all drawn from real life. Like when they put the fellas in a cage and sent them down under water and the shark came and attacked them. That's all happened in real life. I've seen that on the telly.'

'Right,' Mam said. She was looking at me. 'Did you enjoy it?'

'The fella's head came off! The head dropped out of the bottom of the boat with no eyes! It was dead!'

I must have looked pretty scared still.

Mam rounded on Dad and told him off.

I was still going on. 'The shark bit his legs off! Blood was coming out of his mouth!'

Mam yelled at Dad. 'What were you thinking of?'

He'd bought me the poster of the film to stick on the back of my bedroom door. The huge shark's head, all triangular, with twisted jagged teeth. The poor dwarfy girl doing the front crawl at the top of the sea.

The poster glowed in the dark and I sat up in bed, terrified.

Actually, *Jaws* was the only novel I ever saw my Big Nanna reading. She wouldn't go to see the film because she didn't like blood. She thought the book was marvellous. One of her pals from bingo had lent it to her and she kept it in her shopping bag for months. She would pull it out in queues and at bus stops at any moment and immerse herself in it.

Most of the women in our family were big on reading. Dad never was. He thought outdoor pursuits were the thing. Keep yourself fit. Get some fresh air.

Mam would sigh. 'It's because he wanted to be a PE teacher. He had a place at college and everything. Then you came along,' she told me. 'And he had to become a copper at the last minute.'

I would watch the women reading whenever they got a spare moment. They read big, thick romantic novels. Books as thick as a brick, full of danger and forbidden love. They would sit, holding their breath and reading. Often they would have novels set in the North-East, by a lady novelist called Ada Jones.

'She's written over a hundred books,' Mam told me. 'She lived on the same street as your great-grandma, years ago in South Shields, when it was all cobbles and little terraces down by the docks. They're all real life and about real people and how poor everyone was in the olden days.' Then Mam would add, 'Now she's a multi-millionaire, of course. But she gives a lot of her money away to charity.'

At five, six, seven years old, I was thinking that a writer's life seemed quite a good idea.

All these talkative women would sit down and listen to what the ancient Ada Jones said in her books. They didn't listen to anyone else.

It was my Big Nanna who taught me to read, and my Little Nanna who taught me to swear.

I was tiny when my Big Nanna sat reading to me at bedtime. We'd go through book after book and I'd beg for more stories and, for a while, she would give in. As she went along, though, she would change things, especially if she thought the story had taken a nasty turn.

'Well, I think that's bally awful. That's teaching kids wrong.'

Like when Noddy had his car nicked by the Golliwogs in the dark, dark woods and they stripped all his clothes off him and made him crawl back to Big Ears's house on his hands and knees.

'I don't think that's very nice,' she said, and promptly started to change the story.

I knew that I had learned to read when I realised that my Big Nanna was making up her own words. I was reading the real words as she told her own version.

Eventually she would start holding her throat and say, 'I can't go on! I've lost my voice!' She put on this hoarse, rasping voice, but I knew she was pretending.

'One more! Read one more!'

I found out that I could keep her going on longer at bedtime if I got her on to talking about real people. If I got her to tell real-life stories about people in the family, she would stay sitting there on the corner of my bed till the middle of the night. She loved to gossip. My Big Nanna would forget that she had lost her voice and rattle on and on.

Often she'd be complaining about my dad's family.

My Big Nanna sat on the edge of my racing-car bed and said, 'I'll tell you what they're saying about your Little Nanna. It's all true. It's what they're saying down the bingo.'

Both of my Nannas – Big and Little – went to the same massive bingo hall in South Shields. They never spoke to each other these days and everyone knew it. They sat right across the bingo hall from each other.

'They're saying that, first of all, she came from a very rough family in North Shields, a family of thieves and rogues and gypsies, and that all of her seven brothers have been put away in prison.'

'No!' I said.

'It's true,' my Big Nanna said, nodding. She closed the book we'd been reading that night with a resounding bang. It was *Fairy Stories from All Around the World*. This was better, though. Tale-telling.

'It was your great-grandma's sister's daughter who
was telling me, last week. Everyone in the town knows
about her shady past. Her family's famous for being common criminals. Well, you can see that, by what she's like.
Loud-mouthed and rough as guts, underneath it all.
Underneath all the clothes and the jewellery. Well, she
dresses far too young for a Nanna, doesn't she? Your
mam should never have got mixed up with that lot. She's
got herself all involved with criminals and bally gypsies!'

I was amazed. 'I don't believe it!'

'Isn't it a shame?' my Big Nanna said. 'That's in your
blood, that, our David. As well as all the goodness and
honesty from my side, of course.' Then she laughed.

I already knew about the criminals and gypsies. My Little
Nanna had told me a few stories like that, about her own
family. I would sit on the tasselled pouffe beside her gold-
en armchair and she would tell me things. Usually, it was
when she was on baby-sitting duty, when my mam and
dad were having a rare night out at the Chelsea Cat
nightclub in Shields. One time, my Granda was in the
kitchen, putting together a model kit of a battleship.
He'd laid newspaper out on the kitchen table and had all

the plastic bits set out ready with his glue and little pots of enamel paint.

'Eee, is she telling you stories again, bonny lad?' he shouted through. In their living room, the telly was off and my Little Nanna was saying, 'Shall I tell you how my bloody brothers came by a little bit of money? Well, it was when my old granny died and they had to move all of her old furniture out of the tiny house. She'd been in that house 90 bloody years and she had all this stuff squirelled away. Well, my brothers – the buggers – had this little business going. You know, selling things off the dump. What they couldn't sell of my old granny's furniture, they took to the dump.

'Anyway, she had this bloody huge old wardrobe. The kind that people don't have any more. They carried it to the top of the dump between them, all my brothers, and they were going to chuck it off the bloody top, for a laugh. Well, when they did, this huge old thing dropped right down and smashed at the bottom into a million pieces. And guess what, our David?'

'What?'

'It had a false bloody back, all stuffed with money! When the wardrobe exploded, hundreds of thousands of these old-fashioned pound notes burst out like a huge bloody cloud! And they got caught up in the wind and my poor brothers had to go running all over the place to catch them!' And she laughed.

All these women told me stories. They were better than the ones in books that were meant for kids.

Soon, books were something I read alone, by torchlight in the dark at night. And the time with my two nannas and my mam was when they told tales on each other and themselves.

Walking down to Newton Aycliffe town centre on my days off school, Mam would tell me what it was like when we lived with my Little Nanna and Granda, before we had a house of our own.

'Your Little Nanna always wanted to glam up and go out on the town. She would get dressed up to the nines. Your Granda would put on his Homburg hat and suit...'

His hat was all felty and brown and smelled of Brylcreem, though he didn't have any hair left. My Little Nanna would put on her black beehive wig.

My mam said, 'Your dad was doing his police training. We were saving up our pennies, so we couldn't go out anywhere. His parents still took rent off us for living there. We had nothing, when I think. And his parents would come in from their nights out. They'd have been dancing, or at the bingo or playing darts, which they took very seriously. They'd be laughing and smelling of cigarette smoke and sweet booze... Well, I'd have been alone all night in their house... alone with you...

'And your dad, he went out with the other new policemen. Once he came back so drunk that he fell through the glass of the front door and lay bleeding on the front-hall carpet. They laid him in the bath to let the blood run away, until the doctor came. We all stood there looking at him in the bath, everyone standing there in their night-clothes... We were amazed at all the blood and the noise he'd made, falling through the glass... the drunken bloody fool.

'I was standing there, frozen, with you in my arms, looking down at him with these cuts up his arms and all this blood running out. I was thinking, he's going to die, and then what would happen to us? I thought about what your Big Nanna said, that I'd thrown in my lot with his family and I had to stick with them...'

'I think I remember that,' I said. 'Him lying in the

bath and bleeding…'

Mam gave me a funny look. 'How could you?' she laughed. 'You were tiny. You didn't know what was going on.'

But I did remember. I remembered everything I'd seen, and especially everything I'd been told.

5

We're going to Fine Fare. It's the special opening day. It seems like everyone's going down the town centre this afternoon just because this new supermarket is opening in the precinct. The local free paper reckons there will be special offers, a prize trolley dash and a celebrity.

Me and Christopher are walking down town with Mam.

'We might as well see what all the fuss is about,' she says.

We walk down the hill to the burn, over the wooden bridge and up past the school.

When we walk past I can't even look at the driveway leading up to the school. I've got that sick feeling of dread in my stomach, like I have on Saturday mornings when Dad comes to pick us up. Sometimes I wonder, if I just went public with everyone about my super powers, if I just announced all my secrets, they might have to take me out of this school. I'd go to a special one, for other gifted children, like the X Men do. Then I'd be away from the other kids. I'm sure special schools for kids like me must exist.

And I don't mean like the special classes they put on for kids with no ears and who can't read and stuff.

Mam's noticed the look on my face.

'Will Mrs Silone still be there when school starts again?' she asks, knowing that this was my favourite teacher last year. She took us for music and let us make as much noise as we liked. She had us rehearsing 'Kum-Ba-Ya' and 'Send in the Clowns' to sing in assembly. At Christmas we did a play with her – *Peer Gynt*, which was all about trolls. It was different to the usual stuff about Jesus and Cinderella.

'I think she was just there for the year.'

She'd got married. She used to be Miss Lewis, with hair like Barbra Streisand. She used to wear a poncho. She married an Italian man she'd met on holiday and we'd all stared at her, like it was the most daring thing we'd ever heard of anyone doing.

'You used to like her,' Mam says. 'She was better than that Mrs Hellist.' Mam pulls a face. She'd liked Mrs Hellist, with her muddy farmer's wife boots and stringy hair, even less than I did. She used to come to school in a Land Rover and shouted at us all through her nose.

Mrs Hellist used to try to tell me I had to be the same as everyone else in my class. She once took me out into the school hall and told me I had to try harder to be the same. She sat me on the horrible-smelling gym apparatus that was lined along the tall windows and asked: 'Why is it you don't fit in with the other boys, David? Do you have any ideas?'

The gym apparatus reminded me of when she had all of us doing PE in the hall. Everyone was turning somersalts and jumping about all over the place.

I was having trouble with a forward roll. I just could-n't get it right. She nudged me with her toe and said, just to make the others all laugh, 'Oh, come on, you lazy lump.' I flushed bright red. She was getting the others to gather round and laugh. Like I couldn't even do a forward roll.

But she'd never seen me running through the trees. She'd never seen me swinging off branches like Spiderman. None of them knew that I had to play down my powers when I was in public. I couldn't reveal my secret identity.

'It's not a very good idea, you see,' she said, flicking her dirty hair. 'It's not a good idea, being very different

to your peers.' She looked at me. 'Why do you think they
pick on you?'

I sighed and thought back. I chanced an answer. 'It
all started when we first moved into the Juniors, Miss.
And they mixed all the classes up and all that rough lot
came in. Simon and Brian and Duncan Bradley... all the
boys in their gang...'

Mrs Hellist frowned. She wasn't having that. 'I think
really, David, it's down to you, this problem in adjusting.
It's not really their problem, is it? They're just normal,
healthy boys. That's how they are.'

I bit my tongue. I wanted to tell her what they did.
The way they went on. But I knew I couldn't. I couldn't
tell Mrs Hellist about when we went to the swimming
baths on a Tuesday afternoon. Every week for two years
we'd been going, across the school field and the main
road, in a long crocodile, carrying our rolled-up towels
and trunks under our arms.

I couldn't tell Mrs Hellist that the rough boys in the
class were obsessed with each other's dicks. They were
obsessed with getting a glimpse of Mr Goods the swimming teacher's dick, when he changed to instruct us. He
was sporty and young and gave me his towel and trunks

to carry as he led the way to the baths. Simon had been saying that he wanted to see if his dick was as big as Mr Goods's. Simon set great store by having a grown-up-sized willy. They spent a long time changing and showing each other their dicks in the changing room and I kept to one side, trying not to be noticed.

And every week, when they'd got sick of seeing Simon walk around with his towel hanging off his stiff willy or they'd given up hope of Mr Goods coming out of his private changing room to give them a look at his, they'd turn on me. Week after week now I'd been stripped by all the boys in the class. They fell on me each time and ripped off all my clothes and crouched round to stare at my dick. Which was smaller than all of theirs. Well, it's true, isn't it? You get scared and your willy goes up inside of you. And I get in that room of blue tiles and there's just that smell of chlorine and boys and I get scared. And it is smaller. I am different. I don't know why.

Mr Goods must have heard. Even in his private changing cupboard he must have heard them. They were shouting and laughing. They were yelling that I must be a girl. Simon would wave his huge cock under my nose as they all clapped and laughed. He had a bit of towel fluff stuck to the end of it one time and they all reckoned that it must be that spunk stuff. That's the stuff you get coming out of your dick when you get to be old enough. It shoots right out of your dick and they all said that Simon was making it already, at ten, in the changing rooms.

They'd heard all about this sex stuff from older brothers and sisters. I thought they knew too much. It left me confused and worried and scared.

I wasn't turning out right at all.

Of course I couldn't tell Mrs Hellist this stuff. They were rough and they knew too much and they were making spunk and all sorts in the boys' changing rooms and they were yanking off my clothes every week.

'You have to think about this, David,' Mrs Hellist told me in the school hall. Behind us the class, left without a teacher, was going wild.

You could hear them.

'You're going to be stuck with this class, with all these kids, for years to come. You've got years to go with them. You can't stand out as different all your life.'

I looked at her and I knew I was looking fierce. Or that I was going to cry. Hard to tell. I was buggered if I was going to cry.

'You're nothing special,' she told me. 'You're not really different. And that's good. You have to fit in. We all have to. That's how life works.'

'No, it isn't,' I found myself saying. 'I don't have to fit in.'

'Then I imagine you'll find life very difficult,' she said. 'It's you that's in the wrong. Not everyone else.'

I clamped my mouth shut. I'd have to watch what I said to her.

'Life isn't a comic strip, David. I know you think it is, in the silly stories you write for me, but it's not really.'

It was true she didn't much like the stories I wrote in her class. It wasn't fair, because I typed them at home, on the typewriter I got last Christmas. Typed them in red ink because I've worn the black ribbon out. I do pages and pages for her. She just hands them back and gives a look like I'm sucking up to her by doing so much. But I'd be doing those stories at home anyway. She doesn't see them all. Mrs Hellist was always thinking I was just showing off.

Soon after, she led me back to the class and she got on with the lesson about dry-stone walling, which she

was very keen on. She wrote things on the board and we
had to copy them out in silence.

The only part of Mrs Hellist's little talk with me that
I told Mam about was the bit when she tried to put it
down to divorce.

'She said I've got problems relating to the other kids
because Dad walked out on us.'

'She never did!' Mam was scandalised.

'She did. She says I need a male role model in my life.'

'Ha!' Mam laughed, but I could tell she was cross.
'What does she know, anyway?' she shouted. 'That
woman turned up for parents' night with no make-up on
and her hair all greasy. She hadn't dressed up one bit!'

Mam had dressed up for parents' night, of course.
She'd been all done up and ten years younger than everyone else's parents. The headmaster, with his shiny fore-
head and navy blazer, had grinned and slimed around
her. Mrs Hellist had been nasty. Mam gave her a mouth-
ful because she suggested I didn't deserve to be the
brightest kid in the class. If some of the others tried
harder, Mrs Hellist told her, they could be better than
me. Mam told her she was talking rubbish and at that
point we'd left parents' night.

'Bloody common farmer's wife,' Mam had muttered, marching us down the school drive.

That was the end of last year at school. Come September I'll have a new teacher. Both Mam and I are pretty glad about that. I'll still be among the same kids though. But I'm not thinking about all that now. Not really. It's still the summer holidays. And I'm keeping my dread a secret. It's better for Mam if she thinks I think school is OK.

This side of the burn, the houses are older, spaced out more, and they've got driveways for their cars. There are old trees on the pavements and you can see the clock tower above the rec centre in the middle of the shops.

Loads of people are walking down town.

'It doesn't take much to get people excited round here,' Mam says. 'I hope we don't see anyone we know.' She hates bumping into people she knows in the town centre. They stop and get you talking and she blushes and wants to be away. Even the woman who looks after the ladies' toilets chatters away for ages about nothing. That woman waits in her little alcove with a gas fire burning, waiting for people to talk to. Mam says that once, the

ladies' toilet woman had all of her grandchildren sitting
in there with her, eating pasties and sausage rolls. Mam
didn't think that was very hygienic or nice.

'It's like people in this town haven't got anything
better to do,' Mam says, 'other than standing around in
the town centre talking about nothing.'

Mam always says she's shy with other people, but I
can't see how. She says other people, people you hardly
know, always want to know all of your business, and I
suppose that's true enough. 'You have to keep yourself to
yourself,' she tells us. 'Anyway, we don't really belong
here, in this town.'

'Where do we belong, then?' I ask.

'In South Shields!' she says. 'Up there. Not here. We
were just put here because your Dad worked here.'

She'd like to go back to Tyneside one day. The
accents and the way of life and everything is different
here. She talks about being our age and going down the
fair in South Shields, and sitting in booths in proper ice-
cream parlours. They had places where you could sit all
afternoon with ice cream and see all your friends and just
hang around.

The shopping precinct is paved over and pedestrianised. There are ramps and it's on two levels. It's supposed to look dead modern and like something from the future, and maybe it did a few years ago. Now it looks like a tip. The new supermarket is bang in the middle and it's got automatic doors that swish open when people step up to them. That's a bit more futuristic.

'It's the Dalek city,' Christopher says, wide-eyed, watching shoppers going in and out with trolleys and the doors sliding back and forth.

Fine Fare is supposed to sell you everything you might want, all under one roof. It looks packed inside.

'We've missed the opening ceremony, with the celebrity cutting the ribbon,' Mam says as she leads us to the automatic doors.

'It doesn't matter,' I say.

We stand on the sensor pads and the doors slide open for us.

Inside it's all wide aisles and big colour banners showing close-ups of the things for sale. The lights are flickering and fluorescent.

The first thing you see are the toys, records and books.

'You can have your pocket money early if you like,'

Mam tells us with a smile. It's only Wednesday. She's
been saving this surprise up for us.

'Really? Are you sure?' Mam's always saving up these
little surprises for us.

She draws us aside, away from the main aisle, takes
out her shiny purse and pulls out two soft, rolled-up
pound notes. 'I thought you'd want it now, for the new
shop. But mind, it has to last you.'

We thank her and suddenly it's different and more
exciting. The new shop is bound to be full of things we
might want to buy.

We're over at the records and I'm looking at an LP of
superhero themes by Geoff Love and his Orchestra, when
Mam sees Brian coming over. He's in a leather waistcoat
and a soft blue shirt.

'Aren't you supposed to be at work?' she asks him.
She looks pleased to see him.

'It's f-f-factory fortnight,' he tells her.

'That's why town's so busy,' she says. 'I forgot.'

Everyone in the factories gets the same two weeks off,
right in the middle of the school holidays. Everything on
the industrial estate comes to a standstill. You don't hear
that hooter going off at lunch time, the one that sounds

like an air-raid warning. This time of year, everyone in town is on holiday.

'We've just come down to see what's going on,' Mam says. 'Isn't it a posh supermarket?'

'C-c-come over to the f-food hall,' he tells us. 'You'll never b-believe it.'

'What?' she says, calling us over and we follow him.

'My mother,' he says. 'She's only gone and p-p-put herself in for the b-bloody trolley dash.'

It's by the cooked-meats and cheese counter where we first see Brian's mam and dad.

The area is roped off with red cords with tassels, because this is where the trolley dash contestants have been told to wait. Some of them are limbering up beside their empty trolleys. They're touching their toes and stretching their legs.

'They're taking it very seriously,' Mam says. 'How did your mam get herself into this?'

Brian shrugs.

Then we see them. Mam has met them before. We haven't. Brian's mam and dad are still in their outdoor clothes, and this looks odd next to the other contestants.

Some of them are in track suits.

Mam mutters to me, 'Some people will do anything for free groceries.'

A trolley dash is like a race, where you have a certain amount of time to run down the aisles and shove as much stuff as you can into your trolley. The winner is the one whose total comes to the most money. My mam would die of shame if she had to do that with everyone watching.

Brian's mam and dad look older than the others they're standing with. His dad, Arnold, has got white hair, singed yellow by tobacco, and he's got dark bushy eyebrows. He looks embarrassed to be waiting there, where the crowd can see him. His blue coat is zipped right up to his throat, as if he's feeling the chill off the meat freezers.

Brian's mam, Anna, is in a long skirt with boots, a polo neck and a cardigan. Her hair is a glossy black. 'She dyes it like that,' Mam tells me. 'Her and that Maddy Blunt have hair-dyeing sessions together. They drink coffee while it takes, sitting in their bras with towels around their heads in Maddy's kitchen.'

Mam seems to know a lot about Brian and his family.

And I'm surprised to hear her mention Maddy Blunt. John and his mam are supposed to be friends of mine, and quite separate from anything else.

Brian's mam has dark brown sunglasses on, which cover up most of her face. She has a sharp nose and bright red lipstick. She smiles hello at Brian and then starts gabbling away in the strangest accent I have ever heard.

'Oh, haff you heard what zey are making me do? It is ridickerless, iznent it, Brian?'

Brian's dad beside her lets out a long sigh. 'Don't let her fool you,' he says. 'She put her own name down for this. When they called her out over the Tannoy she was over the moon.'

Brian's mam cackles and clutches hold of her trolley, checking that the wheels aren't wonky. Her fingernails are the same dark red as her lipstick.

'Ah, joost let zem try to beat me.' She is sizing up the opposition over her dark brown glasses. Beside the younger, much heftier, women in their saggy track suit bottoms, Brian's mam looks quite nimble and light on her feet. She might be in with a chance here.

'Look,' Brian tells them both. Suddenly he's pointing to where we're standing. He's pointing to us. 'Mary's brought her kids along to watch you.'

This isn't true. We came down to see the new shop. We didn't even know she was doing the trolley dash.

'This is David,' Mam butts in, pushing me forward. 'And this is Christopher.' Chris is more reluctant to be looked at by them.

'Ach, ze kiddies,' smiles Brian's mam. You can tell her teeth are still her own. They've gone a bit yellow with all the cigarettes she smokes.

Her husband looks like he's gasping for a fag.

Both of them still have Australian tans. Under the bright lights of Fine Fare they seem foreign, even before you hear Anna's voice.

'Zese are the kiddies you haff been having your dinners wiz, Brian?' she asks him.

He nods.

'And Mary we haff met before.' She smiles at mam. 'Vot a beautiful family zey are. Very attractif. You haff done well for yourzelf, haznent he, Arnold?'

Arnold smiles weakly, like he really wants to go home.

'Who's the celebrity who's going to start the trolley dash?' I ask, and they all look surprised to hear me talk.

'Oh, joost somebody off ze teevee,' Anna says,

shrugging and waving her hands. 'Off dot local news. I do not recognise him.'

We look across and we recognise him. It's Barry somebody or other, who reads the local headlines at tea time, about strikes and murders and that. He's got a blotchy red face and a hairy-looking suit. He's holding a whining microphone and talking with the other trolley dash contestants, trying to make them line up for the race.

'I will haff to go,' says Anna, looking determined all of a sudden.

'They'll all be heading for the drinks aisles,' Brian's dad tells her. 'It's worth more money, the booze. That's where they'll all go to win.'

'Ookay,' Anna says, and trundles off to the starting line, where Barry the local newsreader is standing with a whistle in his mouth. He pats Brian's mam's shoulder as she pushes past him and she shoots him a look over her dark glasses.

Then we all have to move back, out of the way, into the rest of the crowd. The squawky Tannoy voice announces that the race is about to begin. It is the climax of the opening-day celebrations.

Brian's dad, Arnold, is saying, 'Anna doesn't half get some daft ideas into her head. Did I tell you what she was doing the other day? Only going with that daft Maddy to the priest's house. And posting rolled-up pictures through his front door!'

'P-p-pictures?' says Brian.

'Yes! Those awful religious paintings Maddy spends all her time doing. Well, they're rubbish. And they're rude. Honestly! Shoving mucky pictures through the Father's door! She'll have the coppers on to her!'

Brian's mam is waving to us from the starting line.

Tom the newsreader is shouting out over his mike, 'On your marks! Get set!'

And the contestants brace themselves ready.

Then it's, 'Go!' And he gives a sharp, loud blast on his whistle.

All the trolleys go thundering at once down the clean white lino of the supermarket aisles. All the pushers are hunched over, trotting along as fast as they can. The little rubber wheels make a noise like thunder, almost drowning out the cheering of the crowd. Some of the people around us are shouting out in excitement. None of us is.

'Why does Brian's mam talk funny?' Christopher asks Mam.

'She's Dutch,' she tells him. 'That's just how they talk. Mind,' she adds, 'I think she puts it on a bit thick on purpose.'

All the while, the newsreader is commentating over his mike like it's the football. The contestants have vanished somewhere into the aisles and now we can't see them. But you can hear the crashes and bangs of bottles and tins being chucked into trolleys.

'She'll fall and break her hip bone,' says Brian's dad. 'I did try to warn her.' Then he looks through the crowd and frowns heavily. 'Oh, hell. Oh, no.'

We look to see what's made his face fall. It's Maddy Blunt, her hair an icy white, looking cheerful and dragging John through the crowd behind her.

'Yoo-hoo!' she calls to us.

I haven't seen John since last week. It's a bit weird seeing him with all these grown-ups here. To me, he usually looks like an adult. But with all the others around he seems more like a kid. He's being sulky, too. His hair is greasy and he's hanging his head. He doesn't want to be seen out with his mam.

'Has it started, then, Arnold?' Maddy asks brightly.

'What do you think?' Brian's dad snaps. 'Everyone's

cheering. Of course it's started. You've missed the beginning.'

'Isn't it a marvellous superstore?' Maddy sighs, staring up at the ceiling. She looks just like our teacher did
on our school trip to Durham Cathedral. 'You can get
anything you want here. Anything in the world. It's more
like the superstores we used to go to in Australia, isn't it?'
She nudges Brian.

'Uh, y-yes,' he says.

'Maybe Britain's coming up in the world,' Maddy
says, her smile fading just a bit. 'Maybe it's not such a bad
place to live in after all...'

John has come over to stand by me and Christopher.
We say hello quickly. He's in a black sweatshirt and dark
blue jeans. It's different, talking to each other here, when
there's adults about. So we don't talk. We just stand
together, like kids always do when there's adults about.
The adults push you together as if you're all going to get
on just because you're kids. I don't know what I'd be
saying to John anyway, even if we weren't in a crowd.
While all this is going on, I look at him now and then.

I get a kind of flashback of us lying in the leaves. In a
comic strip there'd be a little box and the editor would

put a note in, saying, 'See last issue, when David and John took all of their clothes off and looked at each other and lay down on the ground under a blanket in order to pass on super powers.' And that would fill in the bit you'd forgotten. Just now it doesn't seem real. John's a bigger boy standing in a crowd with all his clothes on. He's pushed up against me, but it's completely different to before. It's just like anyone pushed up against me in a crowd. I think about how carefully he was touching me. And how different it was to having no clothes on in front of the boys from school in the swimming-baths changing room. When they make me strip they're rough, they pull away the towel I try to cover myself with. John touched me carefully and I never shrunk up inside. I was brave. It was different. But now he's looking at me like I'm just anyone else.

If that's how he wants it I won't say anything. I won't give him a look.

I won't try to remind him of just the other day. But I know what he's like.

I know more about him than anyone else. That's what it feels like right now, right in the middle of Fine Fare. His dick was so hard and so big it could have been fright-

ening. It could have seemed strange and wrong, like the
others' at school. But it never did. It was just John. And
he never said anything about mine being smaller. He just
touched me really gently like he liked the difference
between us. He smiled. Even if nothing like that ever
happens again, I knew that much the other day. I found
out something about him, some secret thing.

We're standing in the crowd with the tense, noisy
seconds going by.

'They must have had longer than two minutes by
now,' Mam says, looking at her watch.

'I w-wish we c-c-could see them,' Brian says. 'It's p-
pointless, this.'

It's true. We're all staring at the counter with the
cheeses from all over the world. We can hear the noise of
the trolley dash, but we can't actually see any of it.

Suddenly the celebrity newsreader starts shouting out
and counting down: 'Twenty! Nineteen! Eighteen!'

People start joining in.

And I decide to try something out.

I squinch up my eyes and concentrate hard.

At my side, John has noticed that I'm up to something and he's looking at me. At last he's looking at me a

bit like he did the other day. His eyes go wider. I've got to do this. I've got to do it now.

I summon up all of my powers and put all of my strength into it. I force my attention out over the grocery aisles like an invisible beam. It's an impervious invisible field of force and I'm projecting it over our heads.

No one can see it. John looks up. He can see it. He's got a share in these powers now. He knows what I'm doing.

I can see all of the contestants dashing about with their half-full trolleys in the last seconds of the dash. And then I find Brian's mam by herself. She's in a right flap, in the booze aisle.

John nudges me, as if he's trying to ask what I'm up to. The pressure on my arm is good. It makes me stronger. I want to look at him. To get him to grin at me again in that lopsided way. But I close my eyes even tighter. I need every iota of my powers to do this. I'm going to bestow upon Brian's mam just a bit of my super-strength and my super-speed.

'Eleven! Ten! Nine!'

My magical force field of influence takes over her for the last few, vital seconds of the competition. Her hands and fingers are a blur as she plucks bottles from the shelves and clanks them into her trolley. None of the others can see this but me. It's working. Anna knows something is going on. She knows that she has been taken over by magic.

I can even hear her thinking, Vot in Gott's name is happening to me?

I can see the thought balloon over her head in the booze aisle as she is bathed in the glow of my force field.

And then, along with all the other contestants, Brian's mam has got only a matter of seconds to get to the checkouts. She steels herself, comes to her senses and prepares for the final dash.

'Five! Four! Three!'

The checkout girls are waiting with ribbons in their hair and rosettes on their new uniforms, ready to tot up and figure out who has dashed and grabbed the most.

'Two!' cries the newsreader over his mike. 'One! You must stop dashing... Now!'

The crowd is moving, surging quickly to the checkout area, keen to see the winner announced.

John is still touching my arm. Under his fingers my skin is burning, though I've stopped using my powers now. I feel his grip loosen and his hand drops away.

'Well,' Brian's dad is saying. 'That was a load of fuss about nothing.'

'Oh, you old sourpuss!' Maddy laughs, shaking out her shock of white hair and leading us along in the crowd. 'It's only a bit of fun!'

Brian's dad glares at her.

'Come on,' Mam tells us kids. 'Otherwise we'll miss it.'

Chris looks quite interested. It's not usual for Mam to be so enthusiastic about something like this. When something like this comes on the telly, she usually reckons it's common.

But now we're moving along, part of the crowd.

John whispers at me, in all the kerfuffle, 'You were using your powers then.' He says it so matter-of-factly. For a second I feel proud. He whispers like he did the other day. Now I can remember what he sounds like when he doesn't want to be heard. His voice broke earlier this year. Now it's kind of chalky and low.

I nod back.

'I could tell,' he says. 'I could feel it.'

'What?' Chris says. 'What are you talking about?'

It would be a nightmare if Chris knew about any of
this. He's like a spy. If he finds out about anything he tells
Mam straight away.

'Nothing,' I tell him, feeling myself going red.

There's a bit of a wait at the checkouts, as the goods
are rung through the tills. There's this electronic noise of
the new tills, all futuristic.

'Well done!' my mam tells Brian's mam. She's standing proudly by her trolley at the till. She looks a bit redder in the face, but she's triumphant as we crowd around
her and watch everything she's grabbed being taken out
of her trolley and being sent down the new, slick convey-
or belt.

Her husband doesn't look too pleased. 'What on
Earth have you gone and got?' he shouts out. Then he's
starting to laugh. 'Look! Look what she's filled her
bloody trolley with!'

Everyone looks.

There are about 30 bright yellow bottles sliding down
the conveyor belt.

'Advocaat!' The old man laughs. 'Bottles of bloody
eggnog! She's got nothing but eggnog! We don't even
like eggnog!'

Maddy Blunt picks one up. 'Oh, I don't know. It's a nice drink. Bit of this and some lemonade and ice. You'd have a Snowball. I love a nice Snowball. It's a very Christmassy drink.'

'But it's August!' shouts Brian's dad.

'I do not know vot came over me...' Brian's mam admits. 'But when dot whistle blew, I knew I joost had to grab as much expensif stuff as I could... It was like I vent into zum kind of trance...'

Then the Tannoy crackles again and the celebrity newsreader announces that Anna has won the opening-day trolley dash.

'I haff won!' she says with solemn satisfaction, as the crowd applauds, her family gathers around her and the newsreader comes over to kiss her.

Later on, after we have said goodbye to them and left Brian to drive his parents home, Mam is saying to me, 'I've never won anything in my whole life. No contests, no competitions. Nothing.'

'Neither have I,' I say.

'But I'm 26!' she cries out.

We're in the garden-furniture bit of the shop. They've

got benches with wide, bright orange umbrellas opened over them. They're set out on yards of plastic grass with fake picnics.

'You'd think I'd have won just one thing by the age of 26,' Mam says.

'We should go in for more competitions,' I tell her. 'Like all the ones in the papers and the magazines. We should send coupons in and write in when they have competitions on the telly...'

On TV shows you usually have to send your answers in on a plain white postcard. Then they put them in a tub and they get someone famous to pull out the winner at random. It looks easy to win.

Suddenly I'm full of plans. We can do anything.

'We'll do every competition going!' I tell her. 'Somebody has to win, don't they? It might as well be us...'

And I'm thinking, I'll put an invisible, powerful spell on every white card we send through the post, to all the magazines and the TV shows. I'll do the same for our answers on a postcard as I did for Brian's mam in the booze aisle. I'll make sure Mam wins something.

'No,' she says, leading us out of Fine Fare. 'I reckon

there's those people who win things like that, and there's
those who never do...'

6

The next thing is Brian's mam coming over to watch telly at ours.

Mam's a bit surprised too, the first time Brian's mam turns up, during the tea-time news, with a Dutch cake she's baked. She's walked across the estate, holding this sticky cake full of currants and fruit upright in an old tin.

'Ach,' she says on the doorstep. 'I called in at dot Maddy's house, but lately she has gone Cattolic again and her zon says dot she has gone to Mass.'

So Mam lets her in.

Brian's mam is wearing beige slacks and a tank top, leaving her brown arms bare. She comes to sit with us on the settee.

'Hello, boyz,' she says to Chris and me. And then she sees the local newsreader on the telly. 'Oh, dot terrible man. Did you see him trying to kiss me when I won ze trolley dashing? I want no men to kiss me in ze public.'

Mam levers the lid off the tin and shows us the traditional Dutch cake Anna has brought. It's in a kind of U shape, with cherries all stuck on with bits of nut and icing sugar like snow.

'Oh, it's lovely,' Mam says. 'Thank you, Anna.'

'Where I come from, it iz only neighbourly to bring sweetmeatz round like dot,' she says. 'Now, I am wanting to know if youz will all be coming to see dot giant spider wid us on Friday night.'

'Well,' says Mam, 'I'm sure the boys are very keen. They like silly things like that. But I really couldn't...'

'There is nothing silly about a giant spider,' Brian's mam laughs. 'What would we do if one came through dis estate, hm? Und it attacked all ze houses?'

This is the kind of thing I think about all the time! I look at Anna in amazement. I didn't think grown-ups ever thought like this.

As the night goes on and we watch *Crossroads*, it becomes clear that Brian's mam is settled in on our settee.

She pulls out her knitting. It turns out she is making a strange-looking hat for the baby that Maddy's ex-husband is about to have with another woman.

'Dot must be a very great pain for Maddy,' she sighs

as the needles click busily.

'Yes,' Mam says. 'It must.'

'To see her huzband running off like dot wiz a mooch, mooch younger woman.'

'Yes.' I can tell Mam is hoping that Brian's mam won't talk all the way through *Emmerdale Farm*.

'But,' Anna goes on, 'sooch is ze way of ze world. And Maddy iz a very wise woman to learn dot lesson. You moost giff in... to ze way dot luff goes. Wiz ze way luff turns out.'

Chris and I look at her. Luff? What on Earth is luff?

'Luff iz vot everyzing is about,' she sighs, rattling her needles. 'Only luff.'

Mam is frowning. 'I suppose so.'

Brian's mam says, 'Maybe, out of all off Maddy's mizery now, zom great good will come out and one day she will be happy.'

'Well,' Mam says, 'we all want to be happy.'

'Or...' Brian's mam goes on, 'she might joost stay very mizzerabel all her life. Who in ze world can say?'

There's a pause then and the adverts come on. The Milk Tray one with the fella jumping off the cliff and fighting sharks with a box of chocolates. The aftershave one with the wife shoving her hand up the bloke's shirt.

Mam says, 'You can never really tell what's going to happen, can you?'

Anna is keeping her eyes on her knitting, peering over her dark glasses.

'Life iz joost ze ups and downz,' she says. 'I bet dot when you married dot husband of yourz you thought dot you would be togedder for edder. No?'

Mam looks shocked for a second that Anna is mentioning Dad. 'Of course,' she says. 'Of course I did.'

'Life turnz out differently.' Brian's mam sighs. 'Und sometimes it iz soo sad. It iz luff behind it all. Luff is very complicated.'

I can still see the day Mam chucked Dad out, clear as anything.

It was towards the end of last year.

He'd taken us out for the morning, down the park.

There'd been rows. But there were always rows. There wasn't any reason to think this was different. But it was building up to something.

When they rowed at night, Christopher and me would sit at the top of the stairs. Just in case it got too bad. Just in case he hurt her.

The day he actually went, there wasn't much of a row. We'd been back from the park for an hour and the house was quiet. Then Dad was calling me downstairs.

When I went down with Chris behind me, he sent Chris back up to our room.

Dad was waiting at the bottom of the stairs and his face was puffy and red and his eyes were pink.

'What's happening?'

He was trying to talk calmly. 'Your mam has told me I've got to move out.'

For a second I'm stuck on the stair carpet, three steps from the bottom landing. For a second I don't know what he's on about.

'She's told me I have to get out and take all my stuff and find somewhere else to live. Away from you and Christopher. And she wants us to get a divorce.'

I still haven't said anything.

He looks at me like he wants me to say something.

'Where is Mam?' I ask.

'In the front room,' he says.

I come down the rest of the stairs and walk through to the front room.

She's there on one of the armchairs. She's got her knees up, her feet off the floor, like the room is flooded and the furniture is floating about.

Dad's behind me in the doorway as I look at her white face.

He pokes me in the back.

'Ask her,' he says.

I look up at him.

'Ask her if I can stay,' he says. 'Ask her if she will let me stay.'

I take a couple of steps across the rug towards her, but something keeps me back.

'Mam?' I go.

She looks up at me.

'Oh, go on, Mam,' I say. 'Let him stay.'

She shakes her head quickly. 'No,' she says.

I realise he's got his hands on my shoulders, squeezing them too tight as she talks.

'He can't,' she says. 'He's got to go.'

'Right,' he says, with his teeth clenched together. I just know without looking that she'll be able to see his teeth clenching, his jaw muscles working, through the sides of his face. 'Right.'

Then he leaves go of me and he's striding off down
the hall and the front door bangs behind him.

I look at Mam for a bit, but she's miles away.

I'll have to go upstairs and tell Chris.

7

The tarmac of the roads round our estate has gone sticky in the sun. It's like walking on sucked and melting sweets. You can smell the creosote they've painted, thick and black, on the fences of our yards. It smells of burning wood and oil and, underneath, the pine is so new, bubbles of sap burst through and you can pick them like jewels. They look like amber.

The dog roses they've planted round the streets have burst into pink flowers. We pick off the orange pods and when you burst them they've got hairy seeds inside. We call them itchybacks and try to shove them down each other's t-shirts.

The trees down the burn are overgrown. It's a mass of waving green. You can hear all the trees from our house at night, making a noise like the sea.

Everyone's playing out. You see gangs from different streets, running around and hanging about in their separate play parks. They come around to see what's going on in different bits of Phoenix Court. Sometimes there's war between the streets, with casualties and battles. Other times we're all down where they're building the boating lake, on the grass between estates. We watch the men digging and pouring cement, which comes out like porridge.

Christopher's allowed to come out of the front yard now, so long as he stays with me. I have to keep a close eye on him. When we go out to play in the afternoon he's taking it all in quietly. He looks amazed, like he's never been out in his life before.

This week we've started playing with Brian's nephews, the Australian kids two doors down from us. Their names are Brett and Allan and they're exactly the same ages as Chris and me, which is pretty weird.

'I think it's better,' Mam says. 'It's better than you playing with that John. He's too old to be playing with you. This is more normal.'

For a second she sounds like Mrs Hellist at school, telling me what's normal when it comes to playing out. I don't tell her this. Mam would go mad, being compared to someone who doesn't wash her hair. But I can't tell Mam that I'd rather be with John. It's something else I just can't tell her.

On these long days on the streets, I don't know where John is, or what he's doing. Probably sitting in his bedroom with the curtains closed and reading his comics. And that's why they call him weird.

I'd rather be in there. Sometimes when I'm playing out with all the kids my age it's like I'm pretending to be a kid and pretending to be having fun. I'm thinking up things for us to do and games to play, but I'm just doing it to fit in. There are other things I'd rather be doing more. When we have races or climb up half-built walls or piles of concrete, I have to really pretend not to have super-strength or speed. To make myself like them. Easier to stay indoors, but that's not allowed on days like this.

What if John came out of his house one day, blinking in the harsh sunlight? And just took me off somewhere? The two of us flying off somewhere. Everyone would be watching from the ground, amazed.

But, as it is, it's long days hanging around the streets, trying to find normal things to do.

Brett and Allan are very brown and have proper Australian accents and long hair. They're like real foreigners, and they can't read or write.

Just imagine that. They don't seem to mind, though. They seem happy enough.

Their garden is full of packing cases, just like Maddy

Blunt's, next door to them. They've got one crate upside
down with a hole cut in one end. It's big enough for
three of us to crawl in at a time. We sit inside like it's a
den. We decide that it's a café and eat stuff in there. Brett
and Allan's mam, Kate, is roped in to serve us hot dogs
and Coke.

The Coke tastes sweeter than usual, and she puts
ribbons of boiled onion and mustard on the hot dogs.
Everything tastes funny in our made-up café. Kate has
made a menu we've pinned up. Inside it's hot and dark
and smells of wood shavings.

But it's not a proper camp, though. When you make
a proper den it has to be in a secret location and you
don't have a grown-up bringing snacks in. It isn't in your
garden. In a way, even as I'm playing with them, I think
it's kind of pathetic that they've got to have a camp in
their garden with their mam acting like a waitress. They
go on like they're wild and out of control and all that, but
they haven't got the imagination to find somewhere
secret, away from the houses and grown-ups. They aren't
really wild at all.

Once we're sorted out in their packing-case den and
the hot dogs are all eaten, it's like Brett and Allan have

run out of ideas for things to do. It gets hotter and
they're tetchy with each other. Then, out come the
Matchbox toy cars. They start playing with cars, having
races. They do all the noises with their mouths and they
race the tiny cars up and down the walls and floor of the
camp. Chris joins in. He's really into it.

This will go on all afternoon. I can't stand playing
with cars.

It gets to be late on on Thursday afternoon. I cut my
losses and scramble back out of their hot and smelly den.
I leave Chris in there and they all carry on with their
races, not even noticing that I've gone.

I sit outside, in their garden, where it's cooler. I'm
cross-legged on the path, reading my way through a heap
of Marvel comics.

I love the way the rough black and white printed
pages seem to drink up the sun and go crinkly and warped
by the end of the day. All four of us love superhero
comics and we've started swapping them. Two British
ones for one of theirs, because theirs are in colour and
therefore worth more. The colours in the American
comics are all tiny dots on the page. If you look too close
in the sun, they can make your eyes swim.

I read superhero comics for the hints and the tips about using your powers wisely. It's sort of like homework for me.

Of course, the British comics aren't as good now, because they've stopped having glossy covers. The stories inside are only like two pages long, too. And they're more expensive to buy! Everything about them has got worse. It makes my older issues even more precious. Of course, I would never say anything like this to Brett and Allan, who are always going on about why their American or Australian comics are best.

That's one thing about all these Australians. Everything they have has got to be the best. Better than anything we could ever have here in England. That's all they go on about. It even gets to Mam after a while. Over there in Australia the sun was brighter, the mountains were higher and the food was nicer. Over here, everything we've got is laughable, and they laugh about it all the time: the way they've come down in the world, just by being here.

John never talks about Australia, though. I don't think he liked it much over there. I'm not surprised. The way they make it sound, it was all about everyone joining in and mixing and being cheerful all the time. Well, I can't exactly see him fitting in with that.

I don't think Mam would, either.

Then Kate, their mother, is coming out to enjoy the baking sun.

She's a big woman, sitting down on the low kitchen doorstep, swaying about a bit as she plonks herself down.

'I thought I'd come out here to work, and keep you guys company.' she grins at me. 'Hi!'

She's not got a scrap of make-up on and her face is freckled and stretched by the sun. She's quite fat and we've been warned not to mention that. Her hair is long and dark, with sunglasses perched on the top of her head. She's in stretchy black pants and a huge Disneyworld T-shirt tight over her massive boobs.

She's come out with a whole load of equipment, and it's this that gets most of my attention as I watch her. There's a short stub of pencil stuck in her mouth and she's placing a battered travel typewriter down on the concrete, between her bare, brown feet. She slaps a heap of typed, scribbled-over pages on the ground beside it and weighs this down with a handy rock. A half-typed page is already hanging out of the typewriter.

I'm dying to ask Brett and Allan's mam what she's doing. I've never seen anyone else typing before. Not outside on their kitchen doorstep anyway, stabbing away at the hard keys with all their fingers.

The keys make a good sound. A rattling, gunfire sound. As Kate batters on, chewing her stub of pencil, the little bell goes off again and again and she's filling up line after line with whatever comes out of her head.

I try to read a bit. I pretend to be reading *The Mighty World of Marvel*, but really I'm looking over her shoulder. The sun is glaring off the white paper. Kate pauses, pops her huge sunglasses on and starts typing away again.

At last she stops and sits back. She gives me a crinkly grin. 'Guess you're wondering what I'm up to, huh?'

'Yes,' I tell her. I'm not afraid of being nosy.

'This is my novel.' She thumps the stack of scruffy, typed-over sheets of paper. 'The whole damned thing. One day I'll even finish it.'

She picks it up, weighing it in her big brown arms. It looks as thick as a mattress.

'I've never met anyone who's written a novel,' I say. 'Is that all yours?'

She laughs. 'Every bloody word! And... before you

ask what it's about – I don't know! All I know is that it's about a glamorous and sexy and chic Australian woman who leaves her husband and kids behind in Wollongong and flies to the United States for an adventure.'

Wollongong is the town where all the Australians used to live. Kate must be writing about herself, I decide. She must be writing about what she really wanted to happen.

'And there she meets up with Starsky and Hutch... you know? Those gorgeous police guys? The dark one and the blond one?'

'It's on too late for us to watch it,' I tell her.

'Right. Well, she hangs around with them and then there are shape-shifting aliens involved, and those guys out of *Star Trek*, Captain Kirk and Mr Spock and everyone, and they all fall in love with the chic Australian lady and – in fact – everyone falls in love with her and she has a wonderful time. What do you think?'

'It sounds fantastic!'

'Oh, well,' she says. 'I'm not making any claims for it as Great Literature or nothing ...'

Her mother, Anna, has appeared behind her in the kitchen doorway, giving us both a surprise. Brian's mam is in a pinny and rubber gloves, and she's carrying a bucket filled with bottles of cleaning things, dusters, polish. Her hair is tied up.

'Dot bathroom of yourz was soo disgraceful, Katy,' she tells her daughter. 'I haff cleaned everyzing. Everyzing from ze top of dot house to ze bottoom.'

'Thanks, Mum,' Kate says, squinching along to let her mother past.

Anna shields her eyes. 'Ach, you have company while you are writing. How iz dot book of yours?'

'It's terrible!' Kate shrugs happily.

Then mam's face appears over the garden gate. She's come out to see that we're OK. She's worrying about us. You can tell by the way she's biting her lip before she says anything.

'I've just come to see that these two aren't making a nuisance of themselves...'

'Hey!' Kate laughs, pulling herself up on to her feet. 'Your two kids are sooo well behaved. Mine run around like two little bastards compared to yours.'

Her two kids come crawling out of the wooden café and Chris is coming out too, blinking and looking like he's about to complain about being taken home too soon. But he also looks glad to see Mam.

'Come on in, Mary,' Kate says. 'Come in and join the gang. Brett, fetch Mary a Coke from the refrigerator. A good and cold one.'

Mam swings open the gate and comes in.

I'm surprised to see her take the bottle of coke that Brett brings out. It's covered in frost with a straw sticking out. Usually she says that Coke gives her a migraine and she can't touch the stuff. She holds it and smiles and there's nowhere for her to sit.

'These two guys of yours are a credit to you, Mary,' Kate tells her. 'I've let mine run wild. There's no controlling them.'

Mam purses her lips, as if she's about to agree. I've heard her say similar things to Brian, about how Kate lets her kids behave really badly and doesn't even mind if they're illiterate.

Brian's mam is bringing out rickety kitchen chairs for all the women to sit on. Kate scoops her heap of typed pages out of the way.

'Hey,' she says. 'Look, Mary, I've got my mum around to do all the housework and stuff. Pretty neat, huh?'

Mam looks at Anna, who is trying to light a cigarette while wearing rubber gloves.

'Your mam does your cleaning for you?'

'Ach,' says Anna, sitting down. 'I yoosed to do it in Australia for her ass well.' She chuckles. 'If I did not do it, our Katy and her huzband and her kiddies would be liffing in a filthy pigs' pit.'

'It's true,' Kate sighs. 'Jeez, I hate cleaning. There's so many more things for a woman of my talents to do.'

As the afternoon goes on and the other kids crawl back into the wooden café and I start flicking through my comics again, Mam is saying dreamily, 'I would love to write a book one day...'

She's staring at Kate's fat brown feet. They're playing with the typewriter keys, which must have gone hot in the sun, the way she keeps twiddling her toes.

'Ah, there's nothing to it ...'

Kate's mother laughs. 'You and dot Brian... both of youz talking for yearz about your novels and your film scripts and your writing for ze teevee... ever sinze you were joost kiddies...'

'I used to be good at English at school,' Mam says.

'But I never got my exams. I couldn't do all the spelling and the grammar and that now… And you have to be able to do all that, don't you?'

'Hey, don't worry about that,' Kate says. 'I don't. Just you write what you want to, sister. Don't let all the rules and all of that get in your way. That's just stuff they make up to stop you doing what you want to do.'

Mam doesn't look convinced. She pulls a face.

'Dot Katy liffs in a world of her own.' Anna laughs. 'She alwayz hass. Look at what she iz writing…' Before Kate can stop her, her mam plucks up a sheet of paper. 'Look at zis!' Her eyes scan down the page quickly. 'All zis sexy nonsense… Dot Starzky and Hootch and zey are… in bed viz each other! And a woman called Kate! Zey are both kissing her! Zey are kissing und kissing und kissing her!' Anna lets out a raucous laugh. 'Katy! Zis is a very rude und sexy story you are writing!'

'Give me that back.' Kate snatches the sheet of paper back. She's blushing red through her tan.

Mam is laughing, shocked. 'In bed? With both Starksy and Hutch?'

Kate starts laughing as well.

Kate's kids start dancing around on the hot

garden path. Brett sings loudly, 'Mum's got a crush on
Starsky and Hutch!'

His younger brother takes up the chant and Chris is
joining in, though he doesn't really understand.

Then Kate is up on her feet in a flash. She slaps both
her kids hard on their bare legs and arms. Her hair's
whipping about and her mood has changed really
quickly.

'Don't you laugh at me!' she shouts. She stamps her
foot on the burning concrete. 'Don't you dare laugh at
what I'm trying to do with my life! Jesus!'

Later, Mam is making our tea.

'Have you seen inside their house?' she asks me. 'Is it
kept nice inside? Is it a mess? What's her furniture like?'

Because it's been a warm afternoon we're having a
light tea. Banana sandwiches. Mam's squashing the
banana down on slices of bread and marge, mashing it
with a fork, sprinkling sugar on top.

'It looked OK,' I tell her.

'Is it as nice as round here?' she asks. 'Is their furniture as nice as ours?'

I shake my head. 'Their settee looks like it's made out

of… like, jeans material.'

'Denim? A denim sofa?'

'And there's loads of stuff lying about. Comics and Action Men with arms and legs pulled off. And –' I pause dramatically – 'I found a crisp packet down the arm of their settee. There were cups with cold coffee in, left on their coffee table.'

I don't feel bad, spreading stories like this. I'm not really slagging Kate off. It's just the little details that Mam likes to know. It's just how we tell stories to each other about other people, with all the little details that bring it all to life.

Mam looks disgusted. 'Fancy having her mam come round to do her housework! And on a hot day like this! She should be ashamed!'

8

We end up going to see the giant spider after all.

We've seen quite a lot of Brian's family this week, so it doesn't seem weird to go out with them on Friday night.

We're going in Brian's yellow Ford Capri and Kate's bringing her car, too. All the way to Darlington, which is ten miles down the motorway.

Chris and I sit in the back of Brian's car. There are sweet wrappers all over the back seat, which is black leather and still hot from the day's sun.

It's weird, being in a car that isn't Dad's.

We both wish Mam had come. I can see it in Chris's face. Sometimes he doesn't have to say anything at all and I know what he's thinking. I don't think that's the super powers, though. I think that's just what it's like to have a brother.

'What are you going to do?' I asked Mam before we left. 'What are you going to do all night by yourself?'

She laughed. 'What do I do all weekend when you're not here? You cheeky thing. There's loads to do. This place is a right mess. I've got a stack of housework to do… ironing and everything.'

Then we went off with Brian. He didn't say anything. He just led us to his car in this funny silence. It was the kind of silence that stops you saying anything between yourselves. It's like that every time he's around.

We're kind of getting used to it now.

Mam says he doesn't really mean to look as if he's in a bad mood all the time. It's just the way his face is.

We sit quietly in the back seat while Brian gets us lost in Darlington town centre. We drive past the Odeon cinema three times as he looks for the big car park.

I get my nerve up. I try to tell him, 'Left here! Down there! It's just round there…'

But he doesn't hear and just gets cross at the steering wheel and we're late for the film starting anyway now.

When we find a space, Kate parks her battered old car just beside us.

'Jeez, you're hopeless,' she tells her brother as her kids jump out and run over to us. Brett and Allan are really excited about this giant spider thing. Sometimes they go on a bit babyish. I mean, it's not like we've come out to see a really big film or something. We're used to going to the pictures. It's nothing new for us. We're there nearly every weekend.

Brian is glaring at his sister, who's combing out her long hair and sighing.

Brian's mam takes charge. 'I think dot film will haff begun without uz...' And she leads the way to the subway under the road.

Mam has given Brian some money to buy sweets before we go in. He's really being like Dad, holding our money for us. We follow him through the double set of glass doors into the cinema. There isn't a queue outside or anything. I'm remembering queueing round the block in Sunderland for *Star Wars*. People we'd never seen in our lives before were talking about the film and how excited they were because it was meant to be so great. Dad had taken us that time and he was just as excited, which was kind of embarrassing. But it was a good day, all the same.

The foyer is empty of other people. It's dark and smells of hot dogs.

Brian queues for our tickets and then he's buying us sweets and he's blushing as he asks for them, stuttering through the glass partition at the woman.

Christopher complains to me: 'He didn't even ask what kind of sweets we want!'

I shush him.

Brian's mam breaks in to tell the woman what he's after.

'Revels?' Chistopher moans. 'Why are they getting Revels? Oh, no. I hate them. Those horrible hard ones you get, and the soft ones that taste like coffee...'

His voice is getting louder. I try to interest him in the new poster for *The Empire Strikes Back*, which is Coming Soon, and which Dad has promised to take us to, but Chris can't be stopped. He's got to, though, otherwise he'll cause a scene. I'm used to his scenes, but the others aren't. It'll be awful if he starts crying. Especially over something like sweets. Brian's family will all think we're spoilt brats. Or we go on weird because our parents are divorced. These are all the things I have to think about when we're with other people. But Chris doesn't have to, because he's too young. He just carries on as normal, being upset at things like Revels.

When Brian and his mam come over, Chris starts asking for a hot dog.

He's pointing at the hot dog counter, where Kate is

buying Brett and Allan the biggest hot dogs in the place.
She's asking for extra mustard, extra tomato sauce and
extra boiled onions. Brett and Allan are looking
really pleased.

'What's the m-m-matter with him?' Brian asks his
mother, looking cross.

'Don't,' I tell Chris. 'Shut up.'

'But they're having them!' he shouts. 'They're having
hot dogs!'

Chris must think he's out with family, or people he
knows, because he's acting like he can't believe it. When
Kate comes over and gives Brian and his mother a hot
dog dripping with ketchup each, Christopher just stands
there stunned.

Brian gives him the packet of Revels. 'Have th-these.'

Christopher holds the packet in both hands. He looks
at it in disgust.

He's right on the verge of bursting into tears. I know
the signs. He's gone red. His eyes are filling up. He's
looking around for someone familiar. He's looking for
Mam.

Instead he sees only me.

The others are wanting to go into Screen One, where

the Giant Spider is already on. You can hear the music through the dark, open door.

Christopher starts to wail. It's one of those long, shuddering, horrible cries of his.

Kate comes over. She's all determined-looking. She looks huge suddenly. Brett and Allan start to giggle. Brian looks furious and worried, holding his hot dog.

Kate fusses on with Chris. At first she's going, 'Oh, sweetheart, what's wrong with you?'

He tries to explain. He's too choked up.

She tries to pull him along, into Screen One, where the others want to be.

But Chris won't move. He won't budge from the spot. I've seen him like this before.

The others all look impatient.

Chris cries even louder, clutching the Revels to his chest. I'm about to say something. I'm about to tell them that I can calm him down. I'm about to explain what it is that's got him so upset.

Kate loses her patience. She slaps him hard on the arm.

He's so shocked, he does as he's told.

And all through the film, as they sit stuffing their

faces, as everyone in the place rustles packets and eats their hot dogs and drinks their drinks and the Giant Spider rampages its crappy way across small-town America and eventually gets blown up and explodes orange, red and black across the wide screen, I'm thinking: she hit Christopher. Mam has got to hear about this.

And I'm planning how to get revenge and how I can muster my special powers without any of them knowing about it. Even sitting here in the dark I can call upon the powers from that other dimension and gather them above the roof of the cinema like pitch-black storm clouds. I could unleash upon them all the most terrible wicked force, all in revenge for Kate slapping Chris.

I could blast all of the Australians right out of existence with a few cosmic thunderbolts smashing down through the ceiling of the picture house. They'd be zapped in their seats and no one would even know that it was me to blame.

And I'm remembering what Maddy said at the same time, though: when you've got mysterious powers like these, you still have a responsibility to the good of mankind. You can't just use them for your own selfish purposes. You can't just go taking revenge. That would make you no better than your average supervillain. That's how, like, Doctor Doom or Kang the Conqueror started off. They were blessed with powers and they used them for the wrong reasons.

And suddenly it looks like I can't do anything but watch the rotten film in the dark and listen to Chris still snuffling in his fold-down seat beside me. He still can't believe that she hit him. And neither can I. And I'm wishing it had never happened and now I'm really wanting a hot dog as well and I know the whole thing will just cause more bother for Mam if we tell her. And then she'll be upset as well, because she thinks we're having a nice time tonight, out with the new family, while she's in and at home alone. She'll think it was all her fault and she wasn't even here when it happened. She'll think that she should never have let us out of her sight.

We get in and it seems very late.

Mam's been sitting up with the telly on, knitting a green jumper from a pattern.

When Brian brings us to the kitchen door, Mam looks relieved and flustered. It seems like years since we've seen her. It seems as long as it does when we come back from a weekend with Dad.

Brian hasn't said a word to us all the way back. But that might not be disgust. That's how he is normally any- way. His mam tried to be kind. She said, 'Did you boys like dot giant spider?'

'You could see it was a car,' I said. 'A car they'd fixed eight legs on and painted to look like a spider.' Then I wince, thinking, 'She might think that's a complaint.' Like I'm thinking the special effects weren't very good. But that's how you talk when you see a film like that. You talk about how real the special effects were.

'A car?' she said. 'Is dot what it was?'

On the kitchen doorstep, Mam asks Brian in for cof- fee, but he's saying it's too late and anyway, he's got his mam waiting out in the car. He's got to drive her home.

Just then, Kate and her kids are walking past our garden, to their own house. Kate must have seen Mam and the rest of us, standing in the lit, open door, but she didn't call across or say anything. She was marching towards her own house, with her bosoms pushed out in front of her.

Suddenly I can see that Mam knows that something has gone on.

Brian's saying good night and going off.

Christopher is all red and bleary as he steps inside, like he might burst into tears again.

'What's wrong with you two?' Mam asks, closing the door on the night. She sounds a little bit scared, even. 'I thought you would have come back happy. What's wrong with your faces? Was the film no good?'

Christopher starts sobbing again, like he's been saving it up. 'It was horrible. It was a horrible film.'

Mam's confused when she sends us up to bed.

I decide not to tell her Kate hit Chris. Not yet.

We're going up the stairs and she shouts after us, 'And get straight to sleep. No talking. You've got a long day ahead tomorrow as well, remember. It's Saturday. Your dad's collecting you at eight in the morning.'

Chris wets his bed.

He gets out of it in the dark and comes over to mine and crawls in. Then he asks: 'Why do we have to see so many people, David? How come we have to see different people all the time?'

9

Mam's up at the crack of dawn. When we come down-stairs she's already playing 'Mull of Kintyre'.

We have our breakfast quietly. Toast and jam and sweet, milky tea.

Mam comes to sit at the table with us. 'Where will he take you this weekend, then?'

'I don't know.'

'The pictures? The swimming baths?' Mam's got that tone in her voice. Like, a bit sarcastic. Like it's Dad's side we're on. Like we already know we'll have a better time with him. Like she can't compete at all. She blows on her tea.

'Is he taking you to stay at your Little Nanna's tonight?'

'I think so.'

'He should tell me his plans. So I know. It's not good enough.'

I ask her, 'What will you do this weekend, Mam?'

She sighs. 'I'll have to go to the shops. Then I'll just be here. Sitting here.'

He's a bit late.

Sometimes before he turns up we've forgotten what he'll look like.

He's in a light blue V-necked jumper and jeans. He's parked on the main road, so he can't hang around waiting.

'Are you ready, lads?'

He always calls us lads. His accent is always a bit more Geordie than we're expecting, like he's come from another country. He talks to us like he's still as familiar. But there's also something in the way he carries on that shows we're as strange to him by now as he has become for us.

Each week he's got a little balder, it seems. Each week he's a little redder in the face. And he talks to Mam like he's never met her before. Nowadays there isn't even that anger in his voice when he talks to her.

Mam's handing us our sports bags with our clothes and stuff in. 'Mull of Kintyre' is coming out from behind her. Dad nods at her.

She tells him not to be late, bringing us back on Sunday.

'Am I ever late?'

'Yes.'

She kisses us goodbye and then we follow him out of

the garden.

He drives us out of Aycliffe. He drives really fast. Mam says coppers drive as fast as they like. They think they're on the telly.

He's driving and he's talking to me. I'm in the passenger seat, and Chistopher's in the back seat, watching everything.

'I thought we'd go straight to Durham. Up to my flat. We'll not bother with the library this week, eh, lads? Forget your books. Then we can buy some of them stickers you like, the ones you're collecting for your sticker books. Have you brought them with you?'

'The football ones?'

'That's the ones. Your FA Cup sticker books I bought you. Have you brought them?'

'Yeah,' I say. 'We brought them.'

'We'll stop in the newsagent's near mine and we'll blow a whole fiver on football stickers, eh, lads? See if we can fill up those books of yours.'

'Yeah.'

I reckon he just likes collecting them for himself. He'd be too embarrassed to buy his own book and collect the stickers for himself, so he got us ours. And he gets more excited about it than we do, when we get back in the car and he opens the packets up, seeing if we got the ones we need to finish our collections. He knows better than we do which are the ones that we've already got. He swaps them with our cousin Martin, who's collecting the same set. I can't really be doing with them. But I make sure both Chris and I have got our sticker books with us, because we know Dad likes them.

All you're collecting, really, when you collect those football stickers, are photos of all these fellas' faces. They're not even smiling. I can't really tell one from the other anyway, though it tells you on the back what their names are and how many goals they've scored.

Footballers aren't really like superheroes. They haven't got powers to set them apart from each other. And they certainly don't wear fancy skin-tight costumes to play in, which is a shame.

Dad really does blow a fiver on these stickers sometimes. He thinks it's a great thing to do. 'Whey, what's money for, eh, lads?' he'll say. But it spoils it, somehow, to get a whole wodge of packets of stickers in one go. Just the other week Mam got us a packet each with the change she had left over from her groceries in town. We still really weren't interested in football or anything, but it meant more, when she pulled these packets out of her bag and gave them to us. She gave us them almost shyly, like stickers was a boys' thing and she didn't really understand. Now it makes me sad and a bit ashamed when Dad talks about blowing a fiver so easily like that.

We've driven out of Aycliffe, into the countryside: the long, flat fields full of swaying yellow corn.

Before we get back on to the main road, he pulls up in a lay-by and stops the engine. He looks over at me.

'Has that Brian moved in with her?'

'With Mam?'

'Has he moved into the house?'

'No!'

'Has he been round a lot? Has that Brian been round every night?'

'No. He's been round for his tea once or twice…'

'Oh, he has, has he?' Dad says. 'That's cosy.'

'And his mam's been round…'

'His mam? What does she want?'

'I don't know. And we went to the pictures with them. *The Giant Spider Invasion.*'

He strokes his moustache, looking at the traffic going by. '*The Giant Spider Invasion,* eh? Did she go with you?'

'Mam stayed at home.'

'She did, did she?'

'Yes.'

'Has she said anything about me? What's she been saying about me?'

'Nothing.'

'Are you sure?'

'Yes.'

He looks at me again. 'You two mean the world to me, you know. You mean everything to me. And you have to remember that I would still be living there, with you every day, if what I wanted meant anything. Remember that. Remember that it was her who wanted me out of your lives.'

He stays quiet for a moment and then he starts sniffing. He looks away and blows his nose.

'Just remember that your dad loves you.'

Then he starts the engine.

'Right,' he says. 'Shall we go and buy some sweets and comics and all the stuff you like, eh, lads? Ha'way, then.'

We drive up to Durham and he puts ELO on his car stereo. He's singing along suddenly with 'Mr Blue Sky'.

'You know, lads,' he goes, 'I reckon if the Beatles were still together, they'd sound just like the Electric Light Orchestra. When you listen to this, it's just... well, classical, isn't it? They've gone... beyond rock 'n' roll.'

ELO are horrible. They've got all these orchestras playing on their records and they've all got big ginger beards. On the front of their record they reckon they live in a spaceship that's orbiting the Earth. But you know it's all lies really.

I've decided that Dad calls it his new flat because that's what everything in it is. There are no funny ornaments on the shelves, no useless bits of things in drawers, no washing left in baskets. The walls are smooth and white, as if the plaster has just dried. The carpets have been recently and carefully laid; no bumps. In his front room the only piece of furniture is a coffee table with a top of smoked glass. It shines. When we come in and Dad flings down his car keys, they land on the glass with a horrible clatter.

Straight away he puts a record on. Jeff Wayne's *War of the Worlds*. It's a recent present to himself. He played it through for us last weekend. It has an open-out sleeve full of paintings of the Martians; of the world being pulled apart.

I take off mine and Christopher's coats.

Dad's head appears around the kitchen door. 'Sausage sandwiches?'

We know he likes them, so I nod. His face is red and puffy-looking, like chilblains. Mam says he looks like that because he's a fat butcher's son. The police force has kept him in trim, but you can't shake off breeding. He's starting to grow a beard and it's thin and spiky-looking. His eyes have gone a watery blue, the skin around them bright red.

Soon there's the sound of a pan spitting; the smell of burning fat.

Christopher sniffs. 'Bits of the new carpet are going up my nose.'

We go for a walk. Dad's new flat was one of the first to be built on this estate. We have to wade through streets of churned mud, the colour of mashed banana, before we come to the countryside. He calls it the countryside, but it's only the fields and woods at the back of the town. We can see the cathedral when we stand on a hump of purple grass. He points it out.

The ponds are rank and brown because it's the middle of the summer. Dad walks with his hand on Christopher's head. His hand is tousling the soft, coppery hair that's grown right over the neck of Christopher's T-shirt.

'She should get it cut for you,' Dad says.

We stand by a pond and listen to the dragonflies agitating. Dad darts forward, clapping his hands suddenly and holding them cupped. 'I've got one!'

Christopher grasps his wrists to see. 'It's smaller than the one in *The Rescuers*,' he says.

I have a look. Its body is soft, segmented in bands of green and purple. Its wings beat a silver sheen to get out. Christopher tuts and walks off to pick some cow parsley. Wherever we go, he always carries back a fistful of cow parsley for Mam.

Dad doesn't know what to do with his dragonfly. You can tell. Its wings are tickling the insides of his palms. He steeples his fingers.

'Should I let it go?'

I'm about to shrug, then I remember not to. He laughs, starts to open his palms, and closes them again.

He's playing a game. Will he, or won't he? Open, close, open. The insect is going frantic. Open, open, closed.

Then Dad's face falls, confused. He spreads his hands to let the insect fly away, but its fat body has popped between his fingers. An orange smear coats the underside of his knuckles. He picks off the emptied bag of its body, grunts and throws it away. He wipes his hands on his jeans.

'Christopher, David... We have to get back. It's time to meet Rachel.'

Dad told me about Rachel a couple of weeks ago. She's his latest girlfriend. I found out about her when I went exploring his bedroom. It looked exciting because it was dark in there, and less tidy than the rest of the flat. A bra was on the floor, stretching itself like a cat under the window.

'Has Mam been round?' I asked, when he caught me there, staring at it.

He said no, it was Rachel's bra. Rachel was the woman up the street. She had a conservatory at the back of her house with potted plants. I could see it if I wanted.

'If Rachel's got a nice house, why does she sleep here?'

He shrugged, forgetting his own rules about doing that. He told me to come and sit on the new, rucked-up duvet. It was a black double duvet with a large, white cartoon rabbit's head on it. I thought that was odd for an adult, but he said it was a present.

'When your mam threw me out... I needed something...' He looked at me. 'You're old enough now. You understand. You're ten. I needed someone. Men... like me... and you... need someone.'

It was a very significant look that he was giving me. Like I was old enough, now, to understand something from the grown-up world. And I knew it's what grown-ups do. You sleep in the same bed. It's like on *Dallas*, when they accuse each other of sleeping with each other and that involves things like going to bed together in the afternoon in bedrooms that aren't your own. They make it seem like an exciting thing to do, like what adults do rather than playing out.

Now I'm thinking of lying under the blanket from John's house. But that was about super powers. It was the ritual. It wasn't just like something normal from the grown-up world. All of Dad's talk of lying in bed with someone must have put it in my mind, though.

Suddenly I can imagine Dad's face if he knew about me and John down the burn. He wouldn't understand. I don't know what he'd say. It's like a happening from a different world, with no place here. It has nothing to do with this, with anything that Dad tells me.

He was saying that men need someone. He was including me in this race of people who grow up to be men and who need someone like a woman. I don't really know what I think about that yet. I don't even know what it means, that Dad talks about women and girls and I don't. It just seems weirder than anything to be under a blanket with a girl.

'So Rachel comes to sleep with you?' I asked. I kept the conversation going. I kept it going so I wouldn't have to keep thinking about myself.

'You'll like Rachel a lot. She knows all about you.'

'What does she do?'

He gave me one of his looks. Sometimes I think he prefers Christopher, because he never asks as many questions. Christopher is easier than me and less complicated; walking around like a monster, growling, occasionally wetting his bed.

'She's a commericial artist, just like Aunty Charlotte. She knows what a good cartoonist you are. She's going to get you a job when you grow up.'

'I want to work for Marvel Comics,' I said, still looking at Rachel's upturned cups. I want to write all the stories and do all the drawings. But that's the kind of job people in America have, where all the comics come from originally. It's not the kind of thing that people do where we come from. But still.

'We'll have to see about that,' he said.

Dad and Christopher have gone for a cup of tea in Rachel's conservatory. Then they're coming back to meet me. I'm not bursting to see her potted plants. Christopher will tell me all about it. He'll like her, probably.

She'll be able to win him over with a KitKat. And she'll fall in love with his dimples.

In the bedroom at Dad's flat that's meant to be ours, I'm sitting on the bottom bunk and ransacking Christopher's *Star Wars* people. Luke, Han and Princess Leia are going through a rough patch. They've left Darth

Vader and the others to sort out the Empire and the Rebel Alliance stuff for themselves. On the duvet Leia is trying to decide between her two four-inch-high fancy men. She hmms and hahs till the two men start to get bored.

I look at the time. What am I supposed to say to this Rachel woman? I've seen your bra? That's what Christopher would say.

A thought strikes me. Han Solo gives Luke Skywalker a brief but impassioned kiss.

This Rachel business means that we won't be going to the swimming baths this week. We get into the police baths for nothing every Saturday. Dad is struggling to teach us to swim. Every week the same.

He'll be undressing Christopher, who will glance around the spartan, tiled room with interest. I hate those places. Dad notices me wearing my towel as a dress, kicking off my clothes. He pulls it away.

'We're all lads together here,' he says crossly, and, to prove it, takes off his own underpants. He jiggles his penis absent-mindedly. It is as worn and red as his face. The grown-up men are the same as the boys at school, looking at each other. I can't believe it. Dad doesn't seem to mind that his willy's smaller than the other fellas'. He stands around and just doesn't seem to care.

Mam tells this story about when I was four and how, together, she and Dad took me to the baths in Darlington. They used to have these tiny cubicles to change in, right by the side of the pool. I went in with Dad and it must have been the first time I saw him naked. I came running out of the door to the poolside, scream-ing my head off: 'It's horrible! It's horrible!' And he came dashing out to grab me with everyone looking at him in the nude. Mam just about died laughing and always does when she tells this story again.

I think I can remember it happening. No, I can. Sometimes it's like Mam's versions of these stories as she tells them replace my own super-powered memories of my own life. But I do remember that; telling the whole world that it was too horrible, the idea of growing up to be a man like Dad, all hairy and everything.

I keep my trunks on in the showers afterwards when we go to the free police baths, standing by Dad as he chats with other naked policemen. I look from one to the next, wondering how they keep from laughing. Quite a few have bigger dicks than Dad. If they're all looking, then I'll look too. Some dicks are like truncheons; defiant-looking, streaming rivulets of soapy water as their owners talk. I wonder how Dad can expose me to this, but he's unaware; scratching his bum, then washing Christopher's hair. I'm getting an odd, hard knot in my swimming trunks that feels like a lump in my throat.

And I am, here now, in the bedroom, playing with the *Star Wars* figures, thinking about the naked policemen, and of lying on the dead leaves with John. This weird, hard pressure in my dick, just like John's. Something that I don't know what to do with. Everything is concentrated there and I don't know what it's for.

Somewhere in the flat a door opens with a clatter. The kitchen blinds are jangling with someone coming in. I hear Christopher's thudding footfalls and Dad's careful voice. I go through feeling strange and red in the face. If I could, I would ask someone what all these feelings mean. What any of them are about. It makes no sense now. It seemed to, the other day, with John. Just for a second. When we weren't saying anything.

Only then.

Rachel is in there, wide-eyed and artistic-looking. She's older than Mam, with a sort of shawl on. Dad introduces us and she's rattling with jewellery when we shake hands. It isn't charm bracelets like my Little Nanna wears. I can't see where Rachel is rattling.

'You're the artist,' she says.

'Christopher draws as well.' I don't want the extra attention just now. But she's looking at me very keenly.

Dad picks Christopher up. 'Aye, all over my glass table!' They laugh.

Rachel sits cross-legged on the new carpet, grinning. We look down at her.

I reckon we should sit down as well, so she won't feel soft. She's getting carpetfluff on her shawl-thing.

'I'm a commericial artist. Do you know what that is?'

I sit across the table and look at how her reflection meets her real body at her boobs. It makes her diamond-shaped.

'You do adverts and stuff in newspapers.'

'And magazines. Full-page spreads, sometimes.'

'Oh.'

'And books. Children's books. I'm what's called an illustrator, really.'

'David reads lots of books,' Dad says, putting Christopher down. He goes to wash out some mugs.

'Oh, yes?' She nudges her elbows on to the table, jangling again. I can see that it's bangles rattling on her forearms. 'What sort of books?'

'Astronomy, evolution and ancient history,' I tell her. 'Do you illustrate those?' I can see her painting cavemen, arranging them round their campfires, roasting their gory dinners.

'Mostly I do story books.' She smiles. 'Don't you like stories?'

Dad's out of the room, so I'm safe to shrug. It's to save him, really, that I do. I don't want to tell anyone that, when he takes me to Aycliffe library on Saturday mornings to change my books, he won't let me choose anything from the fiction shelves. In non-fiction I look for the most exciting things I can. Black holes, dinosaurs and Roman legionaries. It's as close to stories as I can get.

'Have you any of your drawings to show me?'

I tell her no. I don't explain that I always throw them out. Cartoons aren't meant to be kept. In films, fifty-two of them make a second. They are easy to do, and easy to chuck out.

'Get some paper and show her,' Dad says as he comes back in with a tray. There's a bitter smell on the air. His posh new coffee from the bubbling jug. I go off for my book and my felt-tips. Drawing for her will be easier than talking to her. In a flash I know that Dad's drinking that coffee because it's something she has round her house. Something special.

When I come back, Christopher is sat beside Rachel. She's proddng at his dimples with a long index finger. He looks at me in disbelief, slides her a strange sidelong glance, wrinkles his nose and bursts into tears.

'He doesn't like that,' I say.

While they try to calm him down, pressing a KitKat into his hand, I start drawing people from *The Jungle Book*. I've decided to do Walt Disney characters. Grown-ups recognise them easier than they do characters from Marvel comics. The markers make a clean, grinding noise as they slide over the paper.

Rachel jokes with Dad and they tease and tickle Christopher on the floor. He's covered in fluff.

I draw Shere Khan the tiger in jagged black lines. I'm resting on the table, letting the glass shriek under the pen.

Mam will have done her shopping by now. She'll have gone back to the house and it will all be clean, with no one to mess it up. She'll put her groceries away. She could sit still all weekend without moving, until we come back Sunday night, and nothing will change. Then she'll be busy again, for five quick days with us. Time enough to get used to us. And she won't poke her fingers at Christopher's dimples, because she knows he doesn't like it. He doesn't like his cereal, but she would make him eat that. It's for his own good. He'll cry in vicious sobs and all the tickling in the world won't stop him till he's ready to stop.

Dad holds up my drawings for Rachel's inspection. She smiles. She's a commericial artist so, of course, she'll have seen better probably. Dad puts the sheet down and traces the tiger's face with his finger.

'How do you make the eyes so alive?' he asks.

I look at him. It's magic. Does he really want me to explain that to him? It's just another side of my powers.

I can't even start to explain it to him. There's no one I can explain any of it to.

Now he's concentrating on his driving.

The pink tarmac narrows behind us. It's the usual trip to South Shields, with the sky all polished blue over the sea.

'Rachel's got other things to do tonight.'

I thought she might have come with us. She might have stayed at our Little Nanna's, where it's open house for the whole weekend. I want to know what my Little Nanna makes of Rachel. She would grin at her politely and then pull faces behind her back. That would let me off saying anything bad about Rachel, if I could just watch my Little Nanna's reaction instead. She could pick up on the small details and do the laughing and the mickey-taking instead.

We're within sight of the sea. The cliffs drop away to our right and, below them, the water is churning and silvery white.

'What's Rachel doing, then?' I ask.

I'm in the passenger seat as usual, which means I have to talk to Dad. I envy Christopher, who always gets left in peace, sitting on the scalding PVC of the back seat. When Dad takes us home on Sunday nights it's me who has to listen to him. Driving back on Sunday nights he ends up crying. He pulls up in lay-bys to put off taking us back. He cries and asks me questions. I know all the lay-bys between South Shields and our house off by heart.

'Rachel's decorating tonight,' he says.

'Her conservatory?'

'You can't decorate conservatories.' He smiles. 'They're made out of glass.'

'It was a joke.'

'She's doing up her spare room. It's a room for you and Christopher.'

'Oh.' I look out of my window. So we'll have three bedrooms in all. Not counting the one we use at my Little Nanna's.

'I've moved your Scalectrix in there already.'

I'd forgotten about that. It's a black figure eight; a racing track that comes in bits. When it works properly, cars that run on batteries with Velcro fasteners go whizzing round on it. Dad took it with him when he left, so we'd have something to play with during weekends with him.

'I'm planning to move in with Rachel.'

He tells me this very carefully. Like cracking an egg on the side of a pan, teasing the shell apart and letting the yellow heart gollop out. Dad always tells me news like that.

'That'll be nice,' I say. I think for a bit and then I ask him, 'Have you told Little Nanna yet?'

10

When we walk into the butcher's, she's busy serving.

Dad stands at the end of the queue, shuffling sawdust on the pale green tiles. At the glass counter my Little Nanna is telling the whole shop a story and, when Dad realises which one it is, he looks embarrassed. Our Little Nanna always regales the customers in her shop with stories.

'When he came in streaming blood again, I told him, Tom, you either get outside and bash that little bugger into kingdom come, or you don't come back inside this bloody house again.'

She's weighing mince in translucent bags. As she talks she watches the needle quiver on the scales. Then she twists the bags up with Sellotape and sets them down, one by one, on the counter.

She hasn't seen us yet.

'And you know what?'

The customers are like the extras on the telly who never get any lines of their own. They smile and listen expectantly.

'Our Tom went out into the street and gave the little
devil the biggest bloody hiding of his life. And not before
time. I stood on our doorstep and watched until he'd
finished. Later on the mother came round to thank me.
She was a reasonable woman. She thanked me for having
some sense knocked into her boy. That's one pound 34
altogether. Next!'

Then she sees the three of us standing by the stacked
tins. She gives a scream of pleasure. 'There they are!
There's my boys!'

She hunches her shoulders and takes tiny steps around
the counter, pushing through the queue. Her face is one
big grin. She reaches Christopher first and gathers him
up. Her arms are clinking with the jewellery she refuses
to take off for work.

'My kiddas!' she cackles, embracing Dad and me like-
wise.

The whole shop has turned to look. They seem
content to bide.

While Nanna hugs Dad and he mumbles and their
voices dwindle into rapid, adult talk, I notice Granda's
bald head appear over the glass counter. He beams and
nods at me. He gives the counter up to the care of Clive,

one of the ruddy-faced young men, and bustles across to join us. Next thing, he's pressing the usual cold corned-beef slabs into my hands and Christopher's   We like its fatty, metallic taste. Nanna ruffles Christopher's hair and asks if I've been looking after us all.

'And how's your ma?' Granda says. He always asks us this. I think he was fond of her, though he can't say that nowadays.

I'm wanting to ask, 'Do you two know what's been going on with this Rachel woman?'

The queue is thinning. We go through into the back.

There are two more of the young men in the preparation room. More wooden benches, blood and sawdust. Between them the boys have a whole split pig and they're lazily sawing through it as we pass. They look up and smile at us. We're familiar faces, eating handfuls of corned beef, taking everything in.

Another boy in a bloody apron comes out of the walk-in freezer. We get a glimpse of the icy blue forest behind him. It's always dusk inside there. The door seals up with a clicking wheel like a bank vault.

The young men in the shop all have the same look: a speckled, reddened complexion. They smell fresh and bloody, their big hands are stained even when they leave the shop. They look powerful and huge, reaching for the full range of butchery tools.

My Little Nanna calls out to them as she clip-clops through. 'I'm leaving now, boys! I'm off for the weekend with my handsome grandsons! Say goodbye, boys!'

'Goodbye, boys,' the young men chime.

In the smoky office she throws off her apron and busies herself changing sandals for stilettos. 'My feet won't be comfy until they're in agony again.'

A fine dusting of ash lies across every surface. She fishes inside her leopardskin jacket for her Benson and Hedges. She lights one and drags on it happily, like she's in heaven. She closes her eyes and they look completely black in the ill-lit, fly-papered room. 'All that eye make-up,' my other Nanna, my Big Nanna, would say. 'She's always got herself done up like Cleopatra.'

'It's so lovely to see you all.'

Dad stirs. We've been staring at her. 'Shall we go, then?'

She plucks up her handbag, smarms and kisses on some lipstick and fluffs up her jet-black hair. Then she slips a packet of Spangles into my hand, a Milky Way into

Christopher's, and a five-pound note into my pocket for between us, as Dad leads the way out.

She blows smoke through the shop like a runaway train, calling a final farewell to everyone in the backroom and then everyone out front. Granda nods and grins and mouths that he'll see us later.

On the pavement outside she pauses, sucks on her cigarette and then holds it aloft as if testing the wind. 'What about...' she begins, and we know what she's going to say. 'What about Ripon's the toy shop?'

Heels scraping all the way, she leads us up the main road.

Christopher's hand clasped in hers, she calls out to seven separate people she recognises on the way. Dad lags behind us.

They live in a dead-end-road of pebble-dashed houses. Each has a neat, flat garden open to the street, except next door's, which is boxed in with hedges. 'The son's mad as a hatter,' Granda told me once. 'He hangs out of his back bedroom window, taking potshots at freight trains with his air rifle. They should never have bought him it...'

The trains pass the back of the houses every 20 minutes, making the kitchen judder and tinkle.

Each of the front doors in their street is a different colour, the exact shades of Opal Fruits.

Little Nanna has to hurry, she tells us, bouncing out of the car. It's going to be an extra-busy Saturday night. Our cousin Martin is coming to stay. He's the sporty one in the family. Every Saturday he'll be playing on some team or other: football, hockey, cricket, anything. He's in his teens and quite grown up. When he arrives at my Little Nanna's he's always covered in mud, all mussed up and ravenously hungry. She tells us that he'll be here tonight, as soon as his match is over. Every time he turns up I'm disappointed, as if I want my Nanna and Granda just for us.

She makes the gas rings flare into life, bangs the grill pan full of sausages and starts to rub the potatoes clean under the tap, all with her coat still on. She wonders aloud how many goals our Martin will have scored at his football match today.

In the living room Dad is rustling through the *Shields Gazette* for local news. Christopher has gone straight to the telly to wait for *Basil Brush*. I can hear the monotone of the football results. That, with the hissing fat of the chip pan, is the sound of early Saturday night.

I peer inside my Ripon's bag; the six-inch-long stegosaurus glares back at me. My Little Nanna slides a Mars Bar across the table at me.

'While you're waiting for your tea. And get your coat off. Make it look like you're staying.'

The dinosaur is bright orange, with writing embossed on its underbelly. I wonder how prehistoric experts can tell the colours of their hides from old bones.

In Ripon's they keep all the dinosaurs and animals (domestic and wild) in a glass cabinet, like they're jewellery. Different species are set out in ranks. It's all too neat for me. I'd put them in a war or a big picnic. As it is, the brontosauruses arch their necks and gaze into the same distance; the polar bears all put their best feet forward. You make your choice and the cabinet is unlocked by the assistant, who then gropes an arm into the menagerie.

Christopher chose a camel today. He chose a camel last time, too, but he couldn't remember. I know he really wants a giraffe, but anything with a long neck costs double. My Little Nanna would have paid the extra, but we didn't want to push our luck. Besides, it's easier to pretend. A giraffe with a shorter neck is a camel. That's how Christopher looks at it.

Martin is Aunty Charlotte's son. She's a divorcée too. She was married to a miner who lost his job and went crackers, they said.

'Your Little Nanna,' Mam told us, 'stood up in court and told a pack of lies about him.'

The bar in the corner of the front room is stacked with Martin's gleaming sports trophies. One or two tankards, even. On the wall behind them – in a patch cleared of the Airfix model guns Granda likes to make – is a small oil painting Charlotte gave her parents one anniversary. Martin at seven, in football kit, holding a teddy bear. The body is colourful and cartoony, but the face is serious and over-painted. It looks like a photo stuck on, except that one eye is higher than the other.

When he turns up that night Martin goes straight to the lobby at the side of the house to play darts with my Little Nanna. Christopher and I watch *Doctor Who*.

Dad hovers between doors, obviously thinking we

should be joining in more. He always thinks we should be joining in more. 'Come and say hello to your cousin Martin.'

'But Doctor Who's just had himself cloned,' Christopher says. 'Now he's being injected into his own brain.'

Dad gives up and goes to play darts with the others. My eyes are too bad to play. Christopher is too little to be let loose with arrows.

Granda comes in from work with the late football results in the last edition of the paper. Martin pores over them as he eats his extra helpings. Dad, Christopher and I have our tea on the settee off a nest of tables. We watch Martin eat, dribbling bean juice and grease on his tray.

He eats and reads with total concentration.

'You've got to eat!' my Little Nanna says. 'Build you up!'

And when we're finished and really full, then she's pleased. 'Have I won? Have I championed?'

Martin seems too large for the room. He sits in my Little Nanna's armchair and his arms are tucked in like wings. He leans back at last and grins at her and she pats his mop of dark hair. She holds out a glass of his favourite dandelion and burdock. Sarsaparilla they all call it.

'Three goals, he said,' she tells Granda proudly.

Granda is polishing the first in a long line of shoes. Mine, I notice. Whoever visits their house gets their shoes polished before they leave. It's just something my Granda does. Mam did ours this morning, though.

'And he's growing a beard! Look!' my Little Nanna shouts. 'Our little Martin's got a beard coming!'

'No, I haven't.' Martin blushes and returns to scanning the pools coupon.

Once, when I was about five, I pulled my Little Nanna's head off.

It was in this very front room that I did it and I was horrified.

She was sitting in her golden armchair and singing 'Jingle Bells' in the style of Shirley Bassey. It was Christmas and, because there wasn't a Shirley Bassey Christmas carol LP, she was singing along with my Pinky and Perky Christmas record. Just like Shirley, she was doing the quick-quick-slow with the lyrics, hopelessly out of time with the famous pigs, and doing all the waving arm movements.

We had just decorated her tree, which she had kept bare until our visit. She got her grandchildren to do up her tree and she gave out the commands for what went where. First, the glass baubles went on. They were the size of her earrings and were from when Dad had been a boy.

While all the tinsel was going on in golden heaps, I was running about the place. My Big Nanna always says that my Little Nanna gets us kids too whipped up and excitable about Christmas. My Little Nanna always says, 'Oh, what are nannas for, then?'

I kept passing and making grabs at my Little Nanna's curly black hair, over the back of her chair. She must have got fed up and thought to herself: 'Right, I'll fix the little bugger.'

And she loosened all the clips under her wig.

I whizzed past once more and gave it a firm yank.

Off flew her head.

Her glossy black Shirley Bassey wig came off in my hands, the pins and clips flying all over the place.

I screamed and clutched it like a rugby ball and ran full pelt out of the front door. I ran screaming down the street. I ran the length of Chaucer Avenue, yelling as I went. I didn't dare look down at what I had in my arms. I thought I'd see her whole head between my hands. Her face looking up at me.

And when I came back with the wig, what seemed like hours later, they were all laughing. Especially my Little Nanna. Her real hair was flatter and paler. She was throwing her head back and howling with laughter at me.

Then they took a photo of me, out in the wintry street, confused and cradling the Shirley Bassey wig. I'm in a blue cardigan and I've got a knitted orange tie on. I still look a bit shocked. My hair was white then. It's kind of yellow now.

When I wake up I've got no idea where I am.

The curtains are thick and purple and the morning light comes through them only a bit. The room's still dark and the furniture isn't familiar.

I'm on a fold-down sofa bed in the room that used to be Aunty Charlotte's. Some of her things are still in here from years ago. Psychedelic, swirling paintings on the walls. A terrifying clown puppet on the dressing table, and the mirror that glows with this weird, silver light.

Christopher's still fast asleep beside me.

It must be early. The house is completely quiet and still.

I remember falling asleep, I think, on the settee last night. My Little Nanna never tells us when we have to go to bed. We can stay up as long as we like, until we feel tired enough, on Saturday nights. So I stayed up on the settee as the others watched the late movie and then *Match of the Day*.

Fighting sleep, trying to keep my eyes open. I love it when the sounds go fuzzy, like they're coming from under water, and you can still hear the telly going, car chases, guns, american accents and football crowds, and all the family's voices rumbling, cackling on.

Dad was out somewhere last night. Some club, all dressed up, with some other girlfriend in South Shields. I don't remember him coming in. 'Well, he's still young,' is what my Granda said. 'He should be getting out and about.'

My Little Nanna made her usual broth on the stove. Everyone has to have some. It's all lamb and pearl barley. Martin spooned up two bowlfuls and drank sarsaparilla all night.

At one point we all had to stand against the wall so Granda could mark off with a pencil how tall we're all getting. He makes the marks straight on to the orange wallpaper and writes our names beside. We all have our own chart, showing our heights through the years.

Someone must have carried me upstairs to bed. I don't remember going up. I remember the voices going fuzzy and the warm, delicious smell of cigarette smoke. I remember lying in the cool sheets and hearing trains going by in the distance. Then a Shirley Bassey record going on; it must have been in the early hours.

Now, on Sunday morning, the first thing I hear is the Hoover coming on downstairs. Granda is always up first, doing the dishes, hoovering round, making breakfast in bed for my Little Nanna. She sits up in bed with a fur-collared bed-jacket, a tray on her lap and her first cigarette of the day smouldering away. Then Granda puts on his brown hat and goes off to the shop for milk and the Sunday papers.

My mam would go mad if she knew about my Little Nanna's weekend house rules. Like the one about kids staying up as long as they like. The other one Mam would hate is the one about never having to take a bath or wash or brush your teeth. My Little Nanna thinks there's enough time in the rest of the week for all that boring stuff. When they're with her, at the weekend, her grand-children should do exactly what they want to do.

So when I clamber off the bed settee I pull on yester-day's clothes, which are all over the spare-bedroom floor. The pyjamas that Mam ironed and packed for me are still in my sports bag.

'That's what Nannas are for,' my Little Nanna always says. 'Spoiling you rotten. What else are they for, eh? It should all be fun! There's no reason why it shouldn't!'

My mam thinks that can go too far. My mam stopped coming here to visit years before Dad left us. She couldn't bear it here, all the noise and palaver.

Dad's in the bathroom at the end of the hall with the door open and no top on. He's got white lather all over his face and is shaving carefully around his new tash and little, bristly beard. I watch him for a bit before he sees me.

And suddenly I realise, I don't know how, that shaving – this terrible, boring, dangerous thing that you have to do – is going to be something I'll never learn to do properly. Somehow I just know he won't be there to tell me how. And more than that, I don't want him to be.

He swishes the blade in the warm, grey, sudsy water of the basin. How can he do all this with the door open? Shouldn't it be private? There's a line of blood, tiny, on his cheek.

The Sunday papers are out on the kitchen table and my Little Nanna and Granda are brewing up a fresh pot of tea. There's a plate of chocolate biscuits out and that's what we'll probably have for breakfast.

'Eeee, bonny lad,' Granda says. 'You're the first one up.'

We sit quietly as we drink tea, spooning sugar in our mugs. They smoke and rustle the pages of the *News of the World* and the *Sunday People*. The stereo in the front room is playing old-fashioned songs off the radio.

'Is that brother of yours still fast asleep?'

I nod, and can feel that my hair's just about sticking up on end.

'Aw, bless him,' my Little Nanna says.

'They need their sleep when they're growing,' says Granda.

'They're no bother,' my Nanna says, taking the silver-green paper off a minty chocolate biscuit and sliding the plate my way. 'No, the bairns are no bother. Not like the older ones. They're the worry.'

'Eee, pet,' Granda chuckles. 'You're right there.'

My Little Nanna looks at me. 'Has your dad said anything to you about this Rachel woman?'

I nod and start rubbing the sleep out of my eyes. I don't get it as bad as Chris does. Sometimes his eyes get all gummed up in the morning and he can't even open them. 'I've met her,' I say. 'Chris has been round to see her conservatory.'

'Her conservatory, eh?'

And suddenly I decide what I'm going to tell them next. 'Dad reckons he's going to move in with her.' I watch them both take this bit of news in. They need telling. Somehow I can't imagine Rachel sitting round here with them, drinking tea and wearing her shawl. She might look down her nose at them. And they'd be trying to make her feel at home, if they thought she was important to Dad. They'd go along with anything he'd decided. But I still can't see Rachel here. Asking all her questions. She wouldn't fit in at all.

'Well, the bugger!' my Nanna explodes. 'He's never told us that!'

'That's what he says, anyway.' And he was keeping it back from them. He was being dead shifty about it yesterday.

'Oh, leave it be, Eileen,' says my Granda mildly. 'It'll blow over. He won't give that flat up. He's only just got it right. He won't give up his independence so soon. It's just another girlfriend, that's all it is.'

My Little Nanna sighs. 'Aye, just another girlfriend. Well, we all know where that leads, don't we?'

There was a time, a few months ago, when Dad had a different girlfriend every weekend. It was weird. He'd take us out to the pictures or a burger bar and there would be some other woman there, trying to get to know us. We hated it. And we got them mixed up. Once we went to pick up one of these women at her house, and there was last week's woman sat on the settee. It turned out they were sisters.

I told Mam that and she laughed a lot and said she thought it was horrible.

'He's still a young bloke,' Granda says. 'He shouldn't be moving in with another one so soon.'

'Aye.' My Little Nanna nibbles thoughtfully at her chocolate biscuit. 'I think I'll tell him. Tell him what we think.'

'Ah, now, Eileen,' Granda says. 'I don't think you should interfere...'

Oh, now I've started them disagreeing about something. Just by answering a question. This is what always happens.

'Interfere!' she says hotly. 'He's my son! My only son! I've got every right to interfere! His life's been ruined once, we don't want...'

Dad comes in. 'Who's life's been ruined once?'

He's got Christopher with him, looking bleary-eyed, still in his *Planet of the Apes* pyjamas.

Fussing round with Chris and making sure he's got a glass of cold milk and a biscuit take Dad a few moments. There's a kind of stiff atmosphere in the kitchen. It's all my doing, because I spilled the beans about his plans with Rachel. Dad looks at me like he already knows I've been telling tales.

Then my Little Nanna asks Dad, 'What's this David's been telling us? About you moving in with this Rachel woman?'

Dad shoots me a murderous look. 'It... ahm... isn't definite or anything. It's just an idea. I was just telling the bairns... to see what they thought about it...'

My Nanna tuts and she goes to fill up the kettle again with hot water.

'Well, I think you're being daft,' she says at last. 'Jumping straight in with another one. You should enjoy your freedom.'

Chris is sitting at the table, looking a bit worried at the way they're raising their voices. He's never got used to the way they all shout.

'She's a mature person,' Dad says. 'She's got a career, a house. The lads like her.'

My Nanna snorts and turns to me. 'Do you like her?'

'She's all right.' Suddenly I want to say that she wears a funny shawl-thing. That she talks funny, with a kind of lisp. That she tries too hard to get us to like her. And I also realise that I've let them know Dad's secret plans on purpose. I've done it just to cause this scene. If there's a fuss like this, he mightn't move in with her at all. I'm using my mind powers to make things turn out differently.

'It's a funny business, if you ask me,' my Nanna says, and luckily, there's another distraction then, as Martin comes down, yawning, to be fed. He's slept in his football shorts and Newcastle United top.

We don't stay with them for Sunday lunch. Not staying for my Little Nanna's Sunday lunch is unheard of. There's a strange atmosphere in the house and I realise it's because Dad and my Little Nanna aren't talking to each other.

While she's checking the roast in the oven and it's spitting and steaming, all lathered in fat, and Granda's peeling potatoes at the sink, Dad tells them that we're going. He's already slung our bags in the back of his car.

'But your sisters are coming over for dinner,' Granda says. 'They wanted to see the lads. Everyone was going to be together.'

'Aye, well,' says Dad. 'They were going to be, but now they're not.'

'And we were going to have a darts tournament,' my Nanna says, 'and I was gunna mind the bairns while yous went to the pub...'

Dad pulls a face. 'Maybe next time, eh?'

And I'm pleased we're leaving early. Maybe it means we'll get home early. I've done this. I've caused this all to be different, just with a few words.

Dad's in a bad mood when he drives us away, down the empty Sunday streets.

Nanna and Granda came out to wave and kiss us goodbye. They always stay outside their house until we've vanished at the end of the street.

As we leave Shields, Dad's shaking his head and tutting. He looks at me: 'You shouldn't tell people everything.'

'What do you mean?'

'When people ask you stuff, you shouldn't tell them everything.'

'Like about Rachel?'

'Like about anything,' he snaps. 'Some things are private.'

I look out of the window. They're setting a circus up on the wasteground at the back of the crematorium. There are a few scabby-looking camels standing with their coats peeling and dropping off by the tents and I tell Chris to look.

I find it all very confusing, this business of questions and answers.

They all ask me questions and they all want to know the truth. Dad says some things are private. I don't even know what that means. I suppose it means they want to keep things secret from each other. But then they tell me everything. And if I go and tell the truth, they all get cross and stop talking to each other. I wish they'd make up their minds.

For a second I start to doubt my own telepathic powers. I know the things that go on in their minds. I'm supposed to. I can read thoughts as easy as Granda can read out the shocking headlines from the *News of the World*. But when I tell them, when I say the stuff they want to hear, it doesn't come out right somehow. They never look pleased to hear the truth about things.

He takes us to a scruffy café in Sunderland. He's told us about this place. They do these all-day breakfasts on huge plates and he says it's really cheap and good value for money.

There are some rough-looking people in here on a Sunday and the tablecloth is really dirty. The small room smells of vinegar and there's a one-armed bandit that Dad reckons we can have a go on if we eat all of our food.

He says he won 50 pounds on there once and everyone in the place clapped him and cheered. The waitress seems to know him. She's got dyed blonde hair tied up in a pony-tail and a grease-stained stripy apron. She writes down what Dad orders for us in a little pad.

'I've ordered the biggest all-day breakfast for all of us,' he says, smiling. His mood has changed again. 'It's a real challenge to eat it all. The winner gets extra pocket money.'

Everything is a challenge.

'I come here when I'm at work,' he says, lowering his voice and glancing around. 'It sets you up, breakfast from here. And sometimes –' he lowers his voice even more –

'I meet my informants here.'

Chris looks puzzled. 'What's that?'

'Criminals,' he says, smiling. 'Thugs and villains. Hard men. There are a good few of those in Sunderland.'

'You meet criminals here!' I say. I don't know whether to be impressed or dead worried.

'And they grass each other up,' he says, unfolding his paper napkin. 'I play them all off against each other. But I'm the one in control. And they all know it. I'm known around here. Even when I'm in plain clothes, like now.'

When our breakfasts arrive, the plates are stacked high with bacon and fried bread and grilled half-tomatoes. The baked beans are seeping over the edge of the plates.

Dad sighs with satisfaction. 'Now, you two, eat up everything. Show your dad what you're made of. There's someone who's just come in that I have to have a little word with…'

He slips over to the table near the fruit machine. There's an oldish bloke in a mac sat there, smoking. While Dad talks to him I catch Christopher's eye and he looks like he doesn't know where to start on his breakfast.

'Do you think he'll take us home soon?' Chris asks.

I'm not really listening. I'm thinking about cafés where you meet criminals to get your information. I'm thinking of a café – a nicer café than this one – where supervillains like the Green Goblin, Doctor Octopus and the Vulture all hang about having their breakfasts and waiting for the heroes to turn up in plain clothes.

12

The really big villains always come from other dimensions. That's something I've learned from Marvel comics.

Other dimensions means, like, countries or worlds that you can't really get to. They're not like America or Australia, which you can get to if you have loads of money or sell all your belongings to buy a ticket on a plane.

They are places where the rules aren't the same as here. The colours might be different. Everything might be black and white, or the sky might be pink. Pigs might rule the world. In Marvel comics they do this thing called the 'What If?' universe, and that's about how things might have been, if everything was different.

The thing is, that there's different dimensions everywhere and usually people can't get to them. They can't travel across to Alternate Universes unless they have special powers. Mr Fantastic can take the rest of the Fantastic Four to the Negative Zone and the Skrull universe because of his stretchy body powers and his scientific genius. The world destroyer Galactus can travel into any dimension because he's got all sorts of mysterious powers, like God.

We go up and down the A1 at the weekend in Dad's car and I sit in the front, and that's enough universe-jumping for anyone, I reckon. It's dark and we can see all the lights of Tyneside and it's time to leave one side of the family and join the other. The different parts, like alternative realities, lie side by side, but they are unaware of each other's existence.

I couldn't imagine my Little Nanna and, like, Brian and Brian's mam and dad and my Big Nanna all in the same room. It's too weird to think about. They're all separate. If they were in the same place, the universe would probably explode.

That's the kind of thing that happens when people dabble with the dimensions.

We stop at the Granada services on the way back, to buy comics. Dad's not keen, because he likes to talk to us and doesn't like distractions. But we can't miss getting the comics at the Granada. It's the best place for them.

We have to go over the glass bridge across the motoway to get to the shop. We like this bridge, with the cars speeding underneath, because it's like that bit in *Star Wars* where they rescue Princess Leia. Chris runs ahead doing blaster noises with his mouth, turning back and shooting us. Dad sighs. He looks tired all of a sudden. He hasn't talked much for a while. As I walk along with him, high over the motorway, I wonder if he'll be too tired to go into his usual scene before he drops us off. I'm wondering what comics they'll have in the shop downstairs, but I'm also getting butterflies in my stomach about the last bit of the journey home to Aycliffe. Dad'll usually go into his crying and interrogation routine somewhere around Ferryhill, giving him a good ten minutes going on at us. If he's got a lot to say, he'll stop in a lay-by round the corner from our estate. That's why we're often late home to Mam.

'Would that Brian buy you a one-pound-50 comic, eh? Would he spend that much on a comic for you, eh?' Dad's almost sneering as we walk back to the car over the gravel. He's rolled my comic up and he's waving it like a truncheon or something.

Anyway, it's not even a comic. It's the Official Comic Strip Adaptation of *The Empire Strikes Back*. I'm amazed we even found it. It's out early and I can't wait to read it. I can't believe the whole story of the film is in there. Meanwhile, Dad's waving it around and looking cross and calling it a comic, like it's the kind of thing that would come out every week. But it isn't, it's a Special, and no wonder it's cost him as much as one pound 50.

I don't understand him. Sometimes he talks to us about *Star Wars* like it's as important to him as it is to us. Last weekend he got really serious, talking about the Force and would Luke ever make the grade as a Jedi knight, and what might happen in the new film. Dad was comparing the whole Jedi knight thing to his police training, and it was really good talking about *Star Wars* like it was all real.

Tonight he's not that bothered about it. He's shouting about Brian as we get into the car and his ears have gone bright red as he tosses the Official Comic Strip Adaptation on my lap and starts up the car.

This is bad. The Granada services are only just south of Tyneside. He's starting to go on about stuff much earlier than usual.

Chris leans forward to take *The Empire Strikes Back* off me, so he can read it as we drive along the motorway.

The lights are yellow, coming in stripes through the car as
we go under them. It gets brighter and darker. He's holding the adaptation up close to his face in the back of the
car, so he can get all the secrets out of it first. He'd better not spoil it for me.

Dad flexes his fingers on the steering wheel. He has-
n't got his safety belt on. His jaw is set and he's thinking.
The muscles in the side of his jaw are moving as he grits
his teeth.

I open *The Mighty World of Marvel*, hoping that will
stop him talking. Because it's different now and everything's printed smaller and all crammed in, it's harder to
read by the dashboard lights. I've really got to squint.

I'm trying to tell myself that comics are still as good
as they used to be, but I don't think they are. I think
they've been spoiled: cheaper, black and white, rough
paper covers instead of the lovely ones. I'd never admit it
to Brett and Allan, but British comics just aren't like they
were in the old days. I carry on reading anyway.

When superheroes are really cross they grit their
teeth. It happens when they're fighting and leaping into
action, or flying through the air. They look all
determined. Their mouths go like square boxes, showing

all their teeth and that's how you know they're in fighting mode. It's when the Incredible Hulk shouts out, 'Hulk smash puny humans!' or the ever-lovin' Thing yells, 'It's Clobbering Time!'

If I could take my eyes away from my comic and look in the front of the car as we drive along, I'm sure that's what Dad's mouth would be like. His eyes would be blazing and burning and turning a funny colour, just like Dr Banner before he has his chemical reaction and transforms into the Hulk and wreaks havoc.

The lady superheroes don't grit their teeth like that.

I keep my head down, reading.

It's the greatest team-up of all time.

Together they must face and do battle with the dread Hate Monger and the wicked Loki!

It's Earth's Mightiest Heroes drawn together from across the endless vistas of time and space and through the weird Negative Zone!

It's all here, True Believers!

Strike, fools! Forget you are allies and destroy each other!

For the Hate Monger commands you! For, where you aspire to power, to the mere trappings of evil... never forget...

That I am Evil Incarnate!
Kill! Kill! In the name of love!
Kill in a world full of hate!

'When you're a policeman,' Dad says out of the blue, 'it's all about proof. Some people are in the right and some people are in the wrong. When you have the right proof, the proof that you need, then it's all quite straightfor-ward. There's a white side and that's good, and that's the side your Dad's on. And there's a black, evil side, that needs fighting and proving in the wrong, and that's the side I'm after. That's the side I'm against. It's like that vicious transvestite over in Ferryhill, interfering with kiddies. I'll get him and that'll be an end to that. Oh, I'll get him and sort him out all right.'

He looks at me and I'm forced to stop reading.

'I'm in the right, you see, David. I'm on the white side. The right side. And it's always like that. Your mam and that Brian...'

He sucks in his breath and turns his attention back to the road. 'Eee, lad. You don't know how much bad they've done. They don't know. They've torn this family apart. They've torn everything to bits. That's evil, you see? That's what needs to be fought. And only certain people can do it. And that's those in the right.'

Dad doesn't stick to the motorway. This is a bad sign. He takes the B roads through the little towns like Ferryhill and Chilton, which are rough, and there's closed shops and kids hanging round the bus stops and phone boxes. Dad's dawdling all the way home.

We're early anyway. He's set off hours too soon. He's wanted to spend the time talking to me, getting it all off his chest, and he likes to do that in the car.

'What would you think?' he says. 'If you were in my position and you found your wife in bed with another man? Someone who you'd played tennis with? You'd go mad, wouldn't you? Anyone would.'

I don't know what he's on about.

'Anyway, Rachel's asked me to move in with her. I don't care what anyone thinks. If they're all against it, or what. I need to be with her. I need to be with someone. It's not right, me by myself. I get in that flat at night and I'm like, what am I doing here? By myself?'

He looks at me. 'Just you remember, it wasn't me that ripped the family apart. I'm not to blame for any of it. We'd still all be together, if it was up to me.'

Then he's asking about Brian again.

'It sounds like he's got his whole family round your house. Like a bunch of bloody dossers. That's not right. Bloody Australians.'

'They're nice,' I tell him. 'They've all been nice to us. They took us to the pictures, and...'

'I,' he says loudly, 'I take you to the pictures, all right? That's what your dad does. You go to the pictures with me.'

We're on the last stretch of fields and farm buildings before getting to Aycliffe. I can't believe we'll be home soon. Back in our own house, watching our own telly.

'You don't need anyone else,' he says. 'You don't need other people coming in. Who are they to you? Just some bloody Australians. What does your other Nanna have to say about all this? Your Big Nanna? She can't approve of all this. She'll have something to say if bloody Brian moves in with you all...'

'We haven't seen Big Nanna for a couple of weeks,' I tell him. 'She's been in Morocco.'

'Morocco, eh?'

'She sent a postcard saying that she's been on a camel.'

He tuts and shakes his head. 'She's a funny one, as well. Married twice. And she ran away from her second husband, remember? She did a moonlight flit when you were just a little bairn. We loaded all of her stuff into a van and moved her to that flat in Jarrow. All without her husband knowing. Well, whatever he was like, that wasn't right.'

'He was evil, though,' I say, thinking back. My Big Nanna was scared of him cause he used to go doo-lally. She had to batter him that time to keep him away from her.

'It doesn't matter. It wasn't right, just nicking off like that and taking the furniture while his back was turned. All the women in your mam's family are like that. Look at her sister – she's divorced. They're all divorced. They can't live with men. They can't do any of it right.'

That thing about taking the furniture niggles at me. Suddenly, without thinking about it, I'm saying, 'But you took our furniture! When you went you took loads of stuff! We came back from school and there was nothing to sit down on.'

He looks at me really hard. 'Did she tell you to say that?'

'No!' I say. 'And you took the fridge as well.'

'That's not you speaking, David,' he says, slowing the car. 'Those aren't your words. That's stuff she's been saying.'

'But you did! You came round with a van while we were at school. You came round with my godfather, Uncle Steven, to give you a hand and Mam begged you not to take everything...'

'I had to have furniture. It's more mine than it was hers. I was the one that worked. I worked my fingers to the bone for you lot. And then she didn't want me. Of course I'm going to take what's mine.'

We sit quietly. He's found a lay-by just outside Aycliffe. Of course we pull over, in the dark, to sit in it. Behind us, Christopher doesn't make a noise. He's really stuck into *The Empire Strikes Back*.

But suddenly I'm talking. I've started now. I've said stuff back to Dad that's been niggling at me. Every time he's gone on like this on these rides home, I've had things that I wanted to say back to him. Things I never said because he was already crying. Now I've started saying them, they're all coming out and I can't stop. It's like my powers are taking me over. Maybe I've got this glowing cosmic light all around me. I bet I have.

'Mam says she begged you not to take everything. And she begged Uncle Steven, she told him he was supposed to be our godfather, she begged him to leave us stuff. You were even taking our toys...'

'So you'd have toys to play with when you stayed with me at the weekend! You wanted to be with your dad, didn't you? You wanted your stuff at his flat, didn't you? Your Scalectrix and your bloody *Star Wars* men...'

'Mam says you wanted the Scalectrix to play with yourself.'

He flushes red. He opens his mouth and pauses. His teeth are small and square, I notice, on the bottom. His top teeth are large and even, like a horses. He says, 'Why are you doing this, David?'

'What?'

'Answering back. Talking back to your dad like this.'

'I'm not.'

'You're parroting back what she's said about me. Do you do this with her, as well? Carrying tales to her, about what I've said? About what your Nanna and Granda have said?'

'No!'

But that's not true. I've said everything they've wanted me to. And they've all asked me questions, all of them.
I thought that's what they wanted. They all want to know
what each other is thinking. That's what grown-ups want
to know, because they don't talk to each other. They
can't, because they're in different dimensions.

'I'll tell you what you are,' he says to me. 'You're a
bloody little hypocrite. That's what you are.'

I look straight ahead at the dark fields and the chim-
neys of the industrial estate beyond. You can just about
see the lit-up square boxes of our estate from here. I
don't look back at Dad. If I looked at him now, then I'd
start crying. And I'm not doing that.

Hypocrite is like a grown-up word. That's the kind of
thing they call each other. It's not what you call someone
who's ten. I'm savouring the word as I stare
at the industrial estate. I'm a hypocrite. My dad's
told me so.

And it makes me feel like a grown-up. As grown up as
any of them. Good.

But I still don't look at him. I won't.

'It's the way she's been bringing you up. The way she
has you talking.

It's all down to her. It's, like, snide and sly, always listening and carrying tales from one to the other. She's bringing you up all wrong. She'll spoil you. You'll grow up wrong. That's what'll happen to you.'

In a way I'm glad he's angry now. He's too angry to start crying and sobbing at the steering wheel. If he wasn't angry and shouting at me we could be here for ages, watching and listening to him cry. Instead, my heart is jumping and I get a cold excitement in my stomach because he starts the engine up, really hard, so the wheels make a roaring noise on the tarmac and he swings us, really fast, with a screech back on to the road.

'Well, she can have you back,' he says, and his voice cracks and goes high. 'She can have you back right now.'

He takes the car into Aycliffe, past the sign that tells you its population is 25,000 and that we're twinned with Perstop in Sweden. The town is quiet, Sunday night quiet, and he's doing policeman driving through all the empty roads to our house.

He parks up in Phoenix Court.

Chris is tired and wary-looking, clutching *The Empire Strikes Back* to his chest, as if he thinks Dad will take it back off him because it cost so much and he's so cross now. Standing outside Dad's blue car, Chris is looking at me with wide eyes, like I've caused Dad to carry on like this.

Dad's got the boot open and he's grabbing up our sports bags. He carries them both for us and marches us quickly from the main road, through the playpark, round to our house.

It seems weird being back. Like we've been away for months. It doesn't seem like our street any more. What if we've returned in the far future, or a 'What If?' universe where Mam doesn't live here any more? Where no one we know lives round here any more.

And when we go to our house, it's dark inside.

None of the lights are on at all.

Dad bangs his fist on the back door. You can't see anything inside there.

He looks at us, amazed.

'She's not in,' he says quietly. 'How can she not be in?'

I look at my watch. 'We're an hour early. She's not expecting us yet.'

'That doesn't matter,' he snaps. 'That makes no odds.

She should still be there, waiting for you. Where the hell is she?'

He looks at us like we ought to know. I've got no idea. Chris shuffles closer to me. Suddenly I'm scared. Something has happened to Mam.

'The bloody bitch,' he mutters. 'The selfish bitch.' He looks at us, weighing our weekend bags in his hands. His jaw clenches and unclenches. 'She'll be out with that Brian. That's what she'll be doing.'

Now I'm sure something is really wrong. Mam never goes out usually. She never goes out in the dark.

Dad's taking our bags and storming out of our yard.

'Where's he going?' Chris asks, and he sounds frightened.

We have to follow him, because he's got all our stuff.

We follow him right round the street, past the play-park, back to the main road.

'Dad?' I call after him. 'Dad!'

He gets in the phone box. He lets the heavy door close on him and he's searching for change in his pockets and jabbing at the dial. He's left our bags on the grass outside and we stand by them, looking at each other.

'What's happening?' Chris asks.

'I don't know.'

Then Dad is shouting into the phone.

'Where's Mam gone?' Chris asks.

I shake my head.

When dad comes out of the phone box he tells us, 'I phoned your Little Nanna. To see what I should do. Your Little Nanna says that your mother should be here. She says, what does she think she's doing.'

I can feel a panic coming on.

Dad's walking away and tells us to follow him. He's walking back to the car. We don't know what to do. We follow.

He opens the car door.

'Get back in again.'

'What's happening?' I ask.

'Don't back talk me,' he snaps.

'What are you doing?'

He flashes me a look. 'I'm doing what your Little Nanna says is best to do. She said to take you back to hers. Back to Shields. There's no one here for you. This is no good. Your Little Nanna will look after you.'

He slings our bags on the back seat. 'Get in.'

My feet are frozen to the ground. Chris is looking to

see what I'll do.

I can't do this. Not back up the motorway. Not all the way up there. No Mam. The whole weekend, all over again. I can't move.

'Get bloody in!' he shouts. 'Both of yous! Get in the bloody car!'

'We don't want to go back,' I say. 'We want to stay here.' I'm using my super-powered voice. My very calm, serious, grown-up voice that everyone has to listen to and obey.

He stares at me. 'There's no one here for you. No one cares. They're too busy running about. They don't want you. They can't even be bothered to be here for you.'

I open my mouth to say something back. To tell him he's talking rubbish, tell him he's a liar, a *hypocrite,* and he's trying to turn us against Mam. But there's a noise. There's a shout from down the main street.

'David! David and Christopher!'

It's Mam's voice. She's coming up the street with a whole load of people.

Dad's hand is on the car door and my shoulder. His head whips around.

'David! Christopher!' Mam shouts and starts to run.

It's just like the cliffhanger at the end of a Marvel comic.

Suddenly everything seems still to me and dead dramatic.

Mam's running up, wearing her long coat and boots. Brian's behind her and looking confused. Kate's with them, with her husband and Brett and Allan. They're all carrying goldfish in plastic bags of water. They've all got balloons. They've all been laughing and talking and walking along, but now they've seen us and Dad and it's surprised them and it's all gone a bit serious. Maddy Blunt is with them and John's there, too, the only one without a balloon. John's looking straight at us. He's looking at me in the middle of this scene. Brian's mam and dad are the last coming along, up the street to Phoenix Court and our house.

Mam is hurrying up towards us. She's laughing, but there's something, suddenly, scared in her eyes. She can see that Dad has been trying to get us back in the car.

Dad says, 'She's got a bunch of bloody freaks with her.'

Dad gets us into the car and slams the door.

He gets into the driver's seat and slams the door.

He turns on the headlights and revs the engine.

Mam and all of Brian's family are lit up yellow as they run towards us.

Mam shouts out to the others, 'It's David and Christopher!'

She runs straight at the car.

Dad revs the engine harder.

'Dad, don't!' I yell in his ear.

He turns round and glares at me. 'Is it them you want to be with? Is that it? Do you really want to be with that lot?'

I stare back at him and look at Mam, who stands in the headlights with the others coming up behind her. I look at all of them, gathered in front of Dad's car. They're staring at us. I want to say to Dad, yes. That's who I want to be with. It's where Mam is. It's where we have to be, where we want to be.

I say to Dad, 'We're getting out.'

I open the door. Mam's coming round the side.

She lets her balloon go and grabs Chris out. She hauls him up and he's starting to cry. I step out of the car.

'We've been at the fair,' Mam's saying. 'I only went out for an hour... You're not due back yet...'

Dad leans across and pokes his head out of the open door.

'Kiss me goodbye, then,' he says. 'At least kiss your Dad goodbye.'

His car is surrounded by Australians.

I can hear Kate's Wollongong twang calling out, 'Hey, it's Tom! Hi, Tom!'

'Kate,' her dad growls warningly. 'Leave them be.'

Brian leads them all off to our house, letting them in with his own key.

Our house lights come on.

We have to kiss Dad while Mam picks up our bags. There's something I should be saying to him. I should be saying more. That's what I've been doing today. I've been talking like a grown-up. But the words don't come. The powers fail me. Mam's got hold of me like I'm just a kid. But for now that feels OK.

Then Dad drives off without another word.

'What was he doing?' Mam shouts, leading us back to our house. 'What the hell did he think he was up to?'

13

It's like a party round ours. On a Sunday night as well.

All of Brian's family is milling about and Mam's making cups of tea and coffee and passing them round and they're all laughing and talking and wondering where they'll put the goldfish they've won at the fair when they get them home. Chris and I don't know what to make of it at all. We've never seen the house so full of people and everything going on. We're sort of stuck in the L-shaped lounge as Brian puts a record on and his mam and dad are sitting down on the settee and Anna's pointing out different things to Arnold. 'Ach, dot wall unit is very stylish, iznent it, Arn-old?'

'Aye,' he goes. 'It is that.'

We're still in our coats, a bit phased by it all.

'I think we're in an alternate dimension, Chris,' I tell him.

He's sticking close by me. Brian is explaining to Maddy Blunt about the record he's putting on. Then she's saying, 'Oh, we have to hear this. Olivia Newton-John singing with ELO? That's a wonderful combination. Oh, turn the volume up, Brian. We all have to hear this.'

In the kitchen Mam is putting sausage rolls onto a tray to warm in the oven. She's really getting into this sudden party thing. Kate is helping her, chattering away, and Kate's lanky, greasy husband is standing by the back door with her kids. We've not seen much of her husband. I didn't know who he was at first, hanging around our kitchen.

'Hey, Mary, if you ever have any real trouble with that ex-husband of yours,' Kate is saying in a loud, bragging voice, 'we'll set my Des on him, yeah? He'll sort him out, won't you, Des?'

Mam's laughing and brushing her hair out of her face as she bends to look in the oven. 'I don't know what he's playing at,' she's saying. Then she comes into the front room, where we're standing still. Chris is looking shocked by everything. Overwhelmed, I think, is the word.

Mam looks pretty. She's glowing and smiling and gathers the two of us up into a hug. She's wearing new jeans and a blue blouse with short sleeves. Chris is looking tearful when she looks at him. 'But what's the matter?' she asks.

He holds up the Official Comic Strip Adaptation of *The Empire Strikes Back*. 'Darth Vader is Luke Skywalker's dad! He tells him he's his real dad!'

She stares at him and then bursts out laughing.

'Oh, thanks, Chris,' I tell him, dead sarcastically.

'What are you on about?' Mam asks.

'It's true! Then he chops Luke's hand off and he falls off Cloud City! It's all in here!'

'You've spoiled it!' I'm shouting at him suddenly. 'You're spoiling it for me! Shut up!'

This is all over the top of Brian's new record. Olivia Newton-John is singing this daft disco song over the noise of everyone talking.

Mam says firmly, 'Come on. We'll take your bags upstairs. Then you can come back down and say good night to everyone.'

'Say, Mary,' Anna is calling out. 'Iz there somezing wrong viz de kiddies?'

'No, no, they're fine. Just over-tired.' Mam starts to move us out of the L-shaped lounge, into the hallway. 'Come on, boys.'

'Ach, zey are tired,' we can hear Anna telling the others, over the *Xanadu* soundtrack LP.

'Poor lads,' says Maddy Blunt, with a heavy, very depressed-sounding sigh. It hits me suddenly that she's dyed her hair black again. Her art must be going badly. Then Mam shuts the front-room door and she's shooing us upstairs.

'If you'd been here this weekend, you could have come to the fair as well,' Mam's saying. 'It's one of those ones that's only there for a week. Brian said I had to go with them all, otherwise I'd miss it. But I've made him promise we'll go again, this week, so you two can come as well.'

'Did you go on the rides?'

'Me? No! Course not. But there's dodgems and a ghost train and those hooky ducks and everything. It's nearly as good as Shields fair. That daft John went on the Wall of Death by himself.'

'He didn't!' I can't imagine it. It's not the sort of thing he'd do.

'He did! They strap them in and spin them round, all these people. Well, Maddy had a fit and she ran up to the man at the controls – he looked like a right gypsy – and she made him stop it early because John looked sick!

Well, John was so embarrassed...'

He must have nearly died. I can imagine Maddy making him look really daft. I get this odd twinge when I think about him feeling embarrassed and sick like that.

Our bedroom's different. We're standing in the doorway and everything seems to be different when she turns the light on.

'I tidied up a bit while you were away,' she says. 'It looks good, doesn't it?'

'Where's the comics? Where's... everything?'

'Brian helped me. It's much better like this.'

'But where is everything?'

'I put a lot of stuff in the cupboard at the top of the stairs. I chucked some rubbish out. You couldn't move in here before. Anyway, we're going to repaint it next weekend. Blue. In fact, we're going to redecorate the whole house, while you're away with your dad next time.'

We put our bags down.

'Get your pyjamas on and come and say hello to everyone properly and you can have a sausage roll,' Mam says.

'I don't really want to be in my pyjamas in front of everyone...'

'Oh, don't be silly. I bet you've been running around all weekend in your pyjamas at your Little Nanna's. Now come on, I have to go back down.' She's heading out of the door again. She stops. 'Oh, and Brian's got a key now. He's moving in with us. It'll be better like this. He might as well…' She looks at us. She's wondering if this isn't all a bit sudden.

She comes to sit on Chris's bed. 'I've told him, though,' she says, more gently, 'that you two will always come first. It's you two first and then it's him. He'll always be in second place and he knows that. And he still wants to move in. It'll be great. You'll see. We can go out more and do things and go on holidays…'

She looks at the two of us, sitting opposite her. We mustn't look exactly over the moon.

'Has your dad been upsetting you?' she asks.

I shrug. It's hard to say, really.

'Has been calling me names? Slagging me off?'

I nod. 'The usual stuff. Asking questions.'

Chris perks up. 'And he's got this horrible ginger woman who wears a blanket.'

'What?' Mam's laughing.

'It's true!' Chris says, smiling, cause she's laughing.

'She had a blanket wrapped round her.'

'It was like a shawl-thing,' I say.

'God,' says Mam. 'Who's he hanging around with?' She sighs and shakes her head. 'I suppose they were all sat round as usual, calling me all the names under the sun...'

'Granda was asking after you' I tell her.

'Just imagine if you lived with your dad, eh?' she says. 'You'd have to be with that common lot all the time. Just imagine what your life would be like. Well, it would be horrible.'

Then Brian's putting his head round the door. I've never seen him upstairs round our house before. 'Uh... are you c-c-coming down, Mary?'

She gets up. 'Oh, hang on...'

The silvery, purple disco music of *Xanadu* and Olivia Newton-John is coming up the stairs behind him, with the smell of hot sausage rolls from the oven and cigarette smoke. It hits me: she's letting them smoke in the L-shaped lounge!

We get a beaker of hot foaming milk each and a smoked-glass plate with a sausage roll. We sit at the dining table with the other kids, and all the grown-ups are talking over the noise of the music. Brian is putting on record after record: Diana Ross, Rod Stewart, Status Quo. He's brought all of his LPs round. There must be about a thousand of them, all stacked up by the wall unit. I never even noticed, on our way in, that the house is full of his stuff.

John is sitting next to me at the dining table. Actually, now that I think, it does look a bit weird, him sitting here with us younger kids. He is quite a bit older. He looks as out of place as Mam says he is. He's daft and soft and he looks like he feels it just now, with sausage roll crumbs stuck in his polo shirt and on his chin.

'Mam says you went on the Wall of Death,' I say.

He scowls and looks round to see that no one is listening.

'I only went on to prove that I could. There were lads down there, from my class at school. I went on to prove I could do it and not be scared. And I was OK. There was nowt to it. Then my bloody mother made them stop the ride half-way through...' He shakes his head. 'They'll have my life now. It won't be worth living...' He sighs and looks at me. He's just how he was in my head. Just how I remember him. Now that we're sat here away from the others, I can see that it's John. His voice is quieter as he talks about the Wall of Death.

It's so weird, sitting in my diamond-patterned pyjamas from Marks & Spencer, talking to him in a room full of all these people. I brush the pastry crumbs off my jacket and realise that my flies are gaping open and my dick's gone hard. It's pulsing like a heartbeat, in time with the Bee Gee's 'Night Fever', which has just started up. It's different to usual, shoving out of the gap in my pants. It's harder than ever and bigger. It's never been like this before and it won't stop. I look up again and John looks quickly away. I get up to take my plate out and I've got to bunch my pyjamas up at the front and I'll have to stay in the kitchen a while, until it goes.

Kate's in there, demonstrating the Breville toastie and waffle-maker her parents have brought Brian as a moving-in present. I just want her to go but she's made herself dead busy. She's laying slices of bread in the sizzling orange machine and closing its jaws, and calling out to me, 'Hi there, David! Are you going to have a toastie? We're trying them out!'

For a while I don't answer, because I've missed out on going to the fair, my comics have been shoved in a

cupboard or maybe chucked away, Brian has come round
with all his gear and his relations, and my dick is probably going to be this hard and this embarrassing for all the
rest of my life.

That's what it seems like, being in our kitchen this
Sunday night.

14

In the morning Brian's making tea to take upstairs to Mam in bed.

That'll be a change for her. I imagine her saying, like my Little Nanna does, 'Oh, I'm a Lady of Leisure!' as she sits up in bed with her mug of sweet tea.

Brian's got a pair of faded, flared jeans and a yellow t-shirt on. His feet are bare on the kitchen carpet. I go, 'Morning, Brian!' as I come in. Mam's told us this is the polite thing to say and I feel grown up when I say it. He goes, 'Uhhnn-nnuuggh,' back to me.

He's making the tea in the cups – like, dabbing the tea bags in the mugs and then slopping the milk in. When he takes the two mugs away he's left sugar sprinkled everywhere. The kitchen surfaces are puddled in milky tea. I give them a quick wipe down with the dishcloth. Mam wouldn't like to see that when she comes down.

I want to go through that walk-in cupboard and get all my comics out. I might have to go through the bin outside in the yard. She wouldn't chuck out my *Mighty*

Worlds of Marvel, surely. She knows I'm saving them. It might cause bother, though, dragging things out of where Mam's put them. She probably wouldn't like it.

It's kids' morning TV for the holidays. It's those old-fashioned episodes of *Flash Gordon* and *White Horses* and *Why Don't You?*, which is that show where kids from Northern Ireland bake chocolate Rice Crispie cakes and tell you good ideas for things to do with the long, boring days of your summer holidays. That's what they always say, but I don't find the days boring at all. This summer's going all too fast. Back to school soon, Mam keeps saying. It won't be long now. I daren't even count up how many days off are left. I'm dreading going back, though I still always say that I like school really.

I take a couple of cold sausage rolls off the baking tray left on the side and head back upstairs, eating them on the way. The living room smells of fags, like my Little Nanna's house. The ashtray on the coffee table is full. It was a present from when my Big Nanna went to Venice, even though Mam doesn't smoke. Brian's jacket is slung over the settee and his shoes are in the middle of the floor, among all the opened-out record sleeves.

When I go upstairs, Mam's bedroom door is shut, but

the door of the walk-in cupboard has sprung open a bit. Probably because it's so full now. Well, if it's already open, then it won't hurt to have a little look in. I keep thinking of my comics and all the bits I've learned off by heart. It's awful, them being chucked away in there. Like maybe that could even rob me of my super powers.

So I open the cupboard.

There's a new clothes rail in there, wedged between the walls. There's a smell like animals and I see that's 'cause Brian's leather jackets are hanging up in there. About 20 of them, in all different colours, with wide collars and square pockets. There's more records all stacked up and heaps of bin bags crammed with stuff: jumpers and dresses, board games and stuck-together Lego.

I try to undo the black bags carefully, but they're tied too tight and I end up ripping into them, by accident at first. They tumble and slump and gradually stuff starts to spill out of the walk-in cupboard, like an avalanche of old belongings. Photos are sliding out on to the hall carpet. I try to gather them up to poke them back and see that they've been cut up. These are all our holiday snaps from our week in a caravan in Ullswater in 1976. All the square pictures are cut in half. Other pictures have jagged, egg-shaped holes cut in, where Dad's head used to be. Mam's gone through them all with her nail scissors. Most of the photos are crumpled and ruined like this.

I start sticking them back in the plastic sacks. And then I find the comics. I can feel the soft, thick, yellowed paper, the shiny colour covers. I reach into the bag, kneeling down, my arm right in there, trying to get a grip, up to the shoulder. I'm like James Herriott on *All Creatures Great and Small*, with my arm up a cow's bum. I'm trying to drag a handful of comics out, rescuing them from the Negative Zone of bin bags.

There's a ripping noise. And there's something in the way, too – some kind of wire, metal thing that they're snagging on. I grab hold of it and give it a firm yank and the wire comes away in my hand with a nasty scraping noise.

I pull it out and I've got this bent wire coat hanger in my hand, holding it up. God, that's dangerous. I could have cut myself on that. Before I chuck it into the darkest part of the cupboard, I look at it again and realise that it's in the vague shape of Basil Brush.

Then I do sling it into the darkest part of the

cupboard, over the rail of Brian's leather coats. Maybe they'll never find it. Bugger, bugger, bugger. The bin bag I've been rummaging in is now tatters and shreds and I can see how many comics are in there. Loads of them. And a whole load of annuals – *Whizzer and Chips, Doctor Who, Battlestar Galactica*. I start stacking them up till I've got a pile about three feet high. There. That'll make a bit of space in their cupboard.

I pick my hoard up carefully and try to jam the door shut again with my foot. There's a reassuring smell of old paper and printed ink.

Then Mam's stood in the doorway of her bedroom. 'What the bloody hell are you doing?'

I open and close my mouth.

'I've only just put all that old junk in there!' she shouts. 'Jeez!'

Mam's saying 'Jeez!' like Kate does now.

'I'm just putting them back in my room,' I say, and start to scoot past.

Mam's holding her breath and counting to ten. 'I don't know why I even bother. Look, get Christopher up, will you? He'll sleep all day otherwise. And come downstairs. There's something going on outside.' She's heading down the stairs, pulling a jumper on over her blouse.

'What? What's going on?'

Brian's coming out of their room, carrying their empty mugs.

'Kids,' she says. 'Kids shouting out in the street.'

'They're p-p-pulling the bloody trees to b-b-b-b-b-b-bits,' Brian says, thundering down the stairs after Mam.

I tell Chris, 'We have to go down because there's something going on out in the street.'

Chris sleeps really heavily. It takes him ages to wake up and he's grumpy when he does. I'm not like that at all. 'Chris is like his dad in that,' is what Mam says. 'And in wetting the bed, too. Your dad still does that. At 28, he still wets the bed! Mind, that's the drink does that.'

Mam always tells this story about Dad coming in drunk and weeing in their wardrobe. He thought it was the toilet. She thought that was horrible and just about the last straw. He weed on all their shoes and Mam had to chuck them out.

I go over to our window to see what's going on. We've got Disney curtains, all white, with pictures of, like, Mickey and Donald on sledges, going downhill.

There's big boys out there, on the grass in front of the houses and the playpark. Brian was right – they're messing with the new trees. They're pulling them off the splints that keep them upright till they're old enough. There's about six big boys shouting, pulling branches off the saplings and stripping them of leaves and twigs. They're making whips and trying them out, slashing them through the air. I know how good they are as whips, those branches, and the sappy smell of your fingers when you tear the leaves off. We make whips just the same as that, when we go round other streets. We wouldn't do it to the new trees round our street, though.

These bigger boys aren't from round here. They look rough. No wonder their arrival is causing such a fuss. They're yelling and shoving each other. They seem to be shouting up at the houses.

Chris has appeared at my elbow. 'What's going on?' he says thickly, his eyes all gummed up.

I realise then. The big boys are shouting up at the Blunts' house. They're shouting at Maddy and John's place. Their shouts are all raucous and distorted and I can't make them out.

I hurry downstairs with Chris.

Mam stops me at the back door. She's stood there in the
kitchen with Brian. Brian's got the kettle going again,
putting fresh tea bags in their dirty mugs. 'Where do you
think you're going?' she asks me.

'They're shouting at John's house, aren't they?' I say.
'What are they doing that for?'

'Just you stay there,' she warns me. 'I don't know
what they're doing. If they carry on and it gets any worse,
I'll phone the police.'

She pushes me and Chris back and opens the door.
Mam stands on the doorstep with her arms folded, all
watchful.

Two gardens down, Kate is out on her doorstep in a
huge nightie with Brett and Allan beside her. 'Hey,
Mary!' Kate calls. 'What's happening?'

'I don't know!' Mam shouts back. 'But the
language is bloody disgusting. Have you heard them?'

And then we can hear one of them – he'll be their
leader – and what he's shouting up at John's house.

'Ha'way, you yellow-bellied bastard! Why don't you
get out here and fight like a man? We're all out here

waiting. You said you could fettle the whole lot of us! Well, now's your chance, you fucking freak!' His jeers dissolve into laughter from his mates.

'Ahh,' Mam says. 'They're picking on that daft John. They must be from his school. Oh, bless him.'

I try to get past again. 'I'm going out,' I say.

'No, you're not,' she tells me sharply. 'I've told you about playing with him. That weird lad. I warned you. Look at what he gets! He gets into trouble! That'll happen to you if you play around with him!'

I'm stuck in the kitchen.

We look on as the big boys range around, whipping their whips and shouting. Others are looking out of their windows, up and down our street. You can see their faces, frowning, at all the windows. All these pale faces and the lads out there, shouting and cackling.

'This is b-b-b-b-b-bloody stup-p-p-p-p-pid,' Brian says, passing Mam her tea. 'We should phone the p-p-p-police.'

'They might get fed up and go away,' says Mam.

If I was the Human Torch right now, I'd shout 'Flame On!' And I'd burst into incandescent orange fire and all my clothes would burn off me and I'd streak up into the sky, soaring in an arc to everyone's amazement, with my hands flat out in front of me like a swimmer in the shimmering air. I'd bear down on these big boys and shoot bolts of flame at them. I'd scare them to death.

'I'm calling you out, John Blunt!' the leader of their gang yells. 'Come on! Come and face it! Fight me, you weird fucker! Show us what you're made of!'

No one's going to stop him. He's standing right in front of John's front gate, shouting his head off while all his mates are snickering. He throws back his shaved head and laughs out loud, knowing that everyone down our street has got their eyes on him through their windows. He must feel great.

'Ha'way! You queer fucking bastard!'

Then the back door of Maddy and John's house is flung open, like someone's had about as much as they can take. Everyone's holding their breath as someone comes outside.

It's Maddy.

She comes pelting out down her garden path holding a scraggy old broom.

Her black hair is wild and all over the place and she looks frightened and furious. She flings open her garden gate and comes out waving her old yard brush about. 'Go on! Go on and get away!' she yells at the big boys. 'I'll be calling the coppers on you bloody lot!' Her voice has gone all high and screechy.

The big boys fall about, screaming with laughter. But I'm remembering what Maddy said the other day. That she's got powers as well. They shouldn't mess with her. They don't know.

'Fuck you,' their leader shouts. 'You bloody old witch!'

She jabs the broom at him, making him flinch and fall back a step.

Mam's gripping my shoulders and we're frozen on our doorstep.

Maddy is bellowing, 'Why do you always have to get at John? Picking on him like this isn't what he needs!'

They're laughing and whistling and shouting back. Maddy swings the broom around in a circle, holding them back like a pack of dogs.

'He's not got many friends!' she shouts. 'He's a lad with no Dad or anything! You should all be friends with him!'

They laugh even louder at this. 'Get back indoors,

you fucking old slag,' one of them shouts.

She looks lost. For a second I think she's going to turn her powers on them, full force and wipe those grins off their faces. But nothing happens.

She's powerless.

The other day she must have been lying. Or maybe I really was controlling her mind. Either way she's just standing there, helpless, with her broom.

'Why don't you all just piss off!' she shouts, and my mam gasps to hear her swearing.

Maddy is almost knocked flat then by John bolting past her. He's come shooting out of the garden gate, head first.

Maddy falls back, shocked, against the fence. Everyone's shocked.

John lets out this huge roar, taking the big boys by surprise.

I'm gripping Mam's arm.

John's just shouted out, 'It's clobberin' time!' And he rushes headlong into the leader of the boys' gang, winding him and knocking him flat.

At first I want to cheer, but the air has gone out of me, too. I want to cheer because now he can show them all. And it's dangerous, because he'll be revealing himself as superhuman and he'll be giving himself away. But it's just like in the comics, when there's no time to change into your special costume and you just have to go for it in plain clothes.

Maddy screams out John's name, as her son and the big lad roll around in the grass.

There's shouting and noise from everywhere. They've fallen in a whole lot of dog shit and they're rolling in it, grappling with each other.

John isn't doing it. He's being fettled by the bigger boy. He isn't doing anything special at all.

'Oh, Jesus man, Brian,' Mam hisses. 'Stop them! Just stop them!'

They're scragging each other in the grass and the shit, locked in this tight hug and both trying to get a good punch in. They're just the same, matched strength for strength, and the other boy has got all his mates with him. John hasn't got any powers at all.

'John!' Maddy screams.

But then John is hidden from view, as the other five big lads gather round, joining in and piling on. They're kicking at him. They're jumping in, dragging him out and beating him.

'Brian!' Mam turns and yells in his face. 'You get out there and break it up!'

He pauses. He does a kind of jerky movement, like a stutter with his whole body. Then, other men are running out of all the other houses to stop the fight. Now Brian goes running out as well. Mam flies over to the phone. She knows the police station number off by heart because of Dad.

I'm out the back door too, by now, after Brian. Maybe now it's my chance to do something. Maybe I can make the difference. I can bring my own powers to bear. Before, something was holding me back, like a force field or a spell, or it might have been my mam, gripping hold of me, and I couldn't get out there to stop them all fighting. Maybe now I'm just too late.

And the big lads are scattering.

By the time all of the men have come out of their garden gates, the boys are running away, laughing, back to where they came from.

Maddy is hunched over John in the grass and he's covering up his face with both bloody arms to make sure that none of us can see him.

15

'Well, that's the kind of thing that can ruin the whole day,' Mam complains. 'Seeing something like that first thing in the morning.'

This is after the police have been round. They spent some time at Maddy's house and then they came round ours and everyone else's who saw what went on.

It was funny having these great big policemen in their uniforms come in our front room. Mam offered them tea and they seemed to know her. We used to go with Dad to the police Christmas parties at the station down town. They'd put on Punch and Judy shows for the kids and everyone got a present.

'It's not right,' Mam was telling them, 'that kids can get away with braying a daft lad like that John. None of us are safe round here. You lot took your time getting here.'

The policemen just took this criticism. Brian stood in the background. He doesn't like the police.

After they went Maddy poked her head round the kitchen door, looking shocked still.

'I just wanted to thank Brian for coming out and running after them lads,' she said shakily. Mam brought her into the front room and Maddy looked like she was going to cry. She looked smaller and older in our front room than she does in her own.

'I've left John in the bath,' she sniffed, sitting down on the settee. 'He won't say anything about it. He's covered in cuts and dog dirt and everything. He won't talk. I had to take all his clothes off him. They're ruined.'

Mam made clucking noises and looked at me. I was waiting for Maddy to thank me too, for running out to see that John was OK. She'd be thanking me if I'd had a chance to get in there and beat up those lads or do anything proper to help. But she was sunk into herself and didn't really notice I was there.

'If there's anything we can do...' Mam said, as Maddy got up with a deep sigh.

Maddy nodded. 'And to think,' she said grimly, 'just last night we were all sat in here and it was like a party. Laughing. Eating toasties. Listening to Olivia Newton-John.'

'Can I go over and see John?' I spoke up suddenly, just as Maddy was going. Mam shushed me.

'He won't want to see anyone,' Mam said. 'He certainly won't be playing out today.'

Maddy shook her head. She looked at me. 'Maybe later, eh, pet?' She smiled at Mam. 'David's a canny friend for him to have. God knows he needs them. Maybe later on today he can come over and see John. I think John'd like that.'

Then Maddy gave me this strange look, right in the eye, as she turned to step out of our house. I don't think anyone else saw it. But it was a hard look. It was like she was blaming me for what happened to John. No, not quite blaming. But she was asking, in that tiny, hard look she gave me, why it had had to be John to get hurt. And why weren't the powers enough.

That was this morning. After that, Mam has tried to make us forget about seeing the fight in the street. We're going out shopping for the afternoon, in Darlington. We're going out like a family goes out, the four of us, and we're going to the Wimpy and everything.

In a way this afternoon is like a Saturday. We're going round a town centre and we get our pocket money early. It's like what Saturdays would be like if we spent them with Mam instead of Dad.

Brian finds the car park in Darlington quite easily this time.

Chris remembers that we were supposed to be going to the fair.

'Can we go tonight? Can we?'

'I think we've had enough excitement,' Mam says. 'Anyway, you don't want to go round there. They're all dead rough on that fairground.'

We're round Brian's parents' house that night, across the other side of the estate. It's the first time me and Chris have ever been here.

Anna is making a corned-beef and potato pie. 'Dis iz my spezility.' She grins, bending down with her hands bandaged in tea towels as she checks on the oven. The air is steamy and smoky and we're all talking about the fight this morning, out on the street.

Their house is shaped almost the same as ours, except they haven't got a feature window and their lounge isn't L-shaped. It's full of old-fashioned furniture, though. They've got an old, dark, upright piano and the heavy ivory of the keys has gone yellow with fag smoke. They've got lace doilies on the dark wood of the dining table and antimacassars draped on the back of the settee. This stuff comes from Anna's family in Holland, from way back. It's all stuff from before the war.

There's a massive painting of a lake by moonlight, where three horses have come down to the shore for a drink. There's an old ginger cocker spaniel called Pup grumping and snooping about the place like he's not used to visitors in his house. Arnold sits in the centre of the lounge in his padded swivel armchair. He looks like the captain of the ship, like Captain Kirk on *Star Trek*, sitting there. He taps his ash in a pedestal ashtray as we all drink tea out of white and blue china cups, waiting for Anna's corned-beef pie. I watched her crimp the pastry round the edges of a plate and dampen the top with cold milk.

'Ach,' Anna says, settling herself in her own armchair. 'Maddy says dot she had to put her John in ze bath. She had to help him. His hair voz all matted wiz ze dog dirt and it was even stuck in hiss ears. It iz all dissgoosting.'

'The poor lad,' Mam says.

'If I'd been there,' Arnold goes, 'I'd have given them what for. The brutal little buggers. They want birching.'

He shrugs and sighs out his fag smoke in a wide blue fan.
We've been told he used to be a commando and wear a
little beret and carry a knife between his teeth. That's
how he met Anna abroad, in the war.

Brian shakes his head. 'There's n-n-n-nothing mu-
mu-much you c-c-can do...'

'Pah,' Arnold says. 'You can knock their bloody heads
together. You can stop them ganging up, six against one.
You should have been out there earlier, by all accounts,
Brian. You could have stopped them. They might have
killed him, a soft lad like that...'

Brian scowls at his father. Mam gives him a
significant look. It's true, though. All the men came running out of their houses to the rescue, but only after the
big lads had done their business and were going anyway.
The men were helping Maddy to carry John indoors
again and talking sensibly and asking if anything was
broken. They were saying, 'It's OK, the little bastards are
all gone now.'

But when all that was going on I was thinking, Yeah,
they're gone now. That's okay for now, then. That's fine
for today. But those big lads are going to be there tomorrow. They'll be there at school when we have to go back.

I thought – they, or others like them, are always going to be there.

And then I thought – and there'll be no one there to stop it. There never will be. You'll always have to look after yourself.

When it comes to it, no one can really take care of you.

Whatever they say, whatever they promise you.

They'll never, ever, really be there.

I'm watching Anna slice the steaming-hot pie. She examines the shreds of pink corned beef and the slivers of onions.

'Itss perfect,' she says.

'It smells wonderful,' I tell her. I'm ravenous suddenly.

I notice the thick paperback book splayed open on top of the fridge.

'Hey, who's reading this?' I ask.

She grins at me. 'Why, I am, David. Did you not know dot I like to read all ze time?'

Brian's mam is half-way through reading the novelisation of *Battlestar Galactica*. I read it last summer and it was fantastic. But I can't believe someone grown up like Anna is reading it as well.

'Oh, I luff it,' she tells me. 'Dose Cylon warriors? Zey are so evil. Zey are teddible, iznent they?'

Then she's putting thick slices of corned-beef and potato pie on blue china plates and I'm helping to take them through.

Later on Arnold is having a quiet word with me, and I'm sitting on a pouffe beside his captain's swivel chair.

He drags on his ciggy and, out of earshot of all the others – Mam and everyone – he's telling me, 'Ah, well, lad, I have to say that I had my reservations, when he came and told us he'd fallen in love...'

'Is that what he said?'

Arnold nods and drags again. 'Aye, he did. Right out of the blue. Like he never had before. He said, Mam, Dad, I've met the girl of my dreams. Well, we were shocked.'

'I bet!'

'And it was your mam,' Arnold tells me. 'He told us, she's married and she's got two bairns, so there are complications. Well, we took a deep breath at that. But I must say,' he adds, 'it all seems to be working out.'

I nod. I'm not sure what I'm nodding about.

Arnold goes on: 'And she's a lovely girl, your mam. We met her then, you see. And we thought she was just lovely. We were amazed. We couldn't think how he'd managed to get someone as good as her. She's a wonderful girl. We both thought that.'

It's so, so weird to hear him call Mam a girl. But I'm giving in to the weirdness of it all. Sometimes it's the only way.

'So we said, well, of course – you've got our blessing. You go for it, son, we said. We'd be glad to have Mary – and her two bairns – as part of our family.' Arnold sits back, satisfied, his story finished, and he stubs out his fag in the pedestal ashtray. 'So we've got two new grandchildren, all of a sudden! Two new bairns! That's great. It's really great.'

Arnold grins at me. He says 'bairns' and all that, because he's a Geordie really, like all of us. I had it explained to me, earlier tonight. Anna and Arnold met in Holland during the war and at first they lived here in the North-East. It was in the 1950s that they went to Australia and there they had Brian and Kate, who grew up on the beach. Now they're back and Arnold fits in 'cause he still has this accent, this easygoing attitude to life. He's familiar. Brian, Kate and Anna all still talk about what a great life they had in Australia, having dinner on the beach and skiing in the Snowy Mountains. But Arnold prefers it here.

The way he goes on, it's not that different to my own Granda. Both him and Anna seem to me like people who could be in my family. I know, really, that they're trying hard and they're being really nice to us. And I'm glad they are. I like them and Mam's smiling at me from across the lounge, because I've been grown up and spoken nicely to both of them.

She likes it when I act grown up like this. But I like talking to people. I like them talking to me like I'm some-one worth talking to.

We sit in all their fag smoke and look at each other and Anna gets the kettle on for another cup of tea and lets their elderly spaniel out into the yard.

I just wish Brian could be like them. I wish he would even try.

When we walk back across the estate the whole place has

gone quiet and still. It's cooler because summer is really going.

We take our time as the street-lights pop on, one after another. We go across the way where they've been building the new boating lake.

'Hey, it's finished,' Mam says.

It's true. They've let the concrete of the lake dry out and they've filled it up with water without anyone even noticing. It's like a clear black sheet of glass, all stretched out in the dark in the middle of the estate. There's a small waterfall and the dark water's thundering down in creamy foam and then spreading out into the wide, new lake.

We go across the bridge and it feels special, being the first ones to step on the new, fresh half-dried cement.

'We should write our names in it,' Mam says, looking back at our footprints. But we don't, because then people could tell who it was.

We get back to our street. To our house. It's Brian's house too, now. I wonder what it seems like to him, walking from his old place in his mam's house, to his new place with us. But, it's like Mam said earlier today – he's far too old to be living there with them. He's 27 now. He's like an old man, to be living at home. His whole new family is ready-made, all sprung up around him, like putting hot water in a Pot Noodle.

We walk home.

I want to call in and see how John is. I want to knock on Maddy's door.

At first Mam looks like she's in two minds because it's dark and too late.

'I want to see that he's OK,' I tell her.

She looks at me, stood at our garden gate. She's looking at me like she's checking that I'll be all right by myself. But I've been grown up all day. She knows I have. She nods.

I rush up our street to John's house.

I can hear Mam, Brian and Chris going into ours and turning on the lights.

I go up the Blunts' front path and I'm knocking on their door.

'Maddy,' I say, when she answers the door in the dark. She's got a dirty paintbrush and a rosary in one hand. She lets me in without a word.

Now it's John lying there on his bed in his pyjamas and it's me who's fully clothed.

He's all stretched out on his single bed and he's got tissue paper, purple and pink, on his lamp, so the light is spooky and dim. Incense is burning, something he says is called jasmine. His horror-film posters look even scarier like this. There are a stack of those creepy 2000AD comics piled up by his bed. He's been lying there all afternoon and evening, flicking through them, and his face has been swelling up and turning purple.

'All my arms and legs are black and blue,' he says, pushing the thick, dark hair out of his eyes. 'I'm a fucking disaster area.'

I'm thrilled to hear him swear like this, like a hard lad. I sit by his bed as he shows me his bruises.

'They were evil to you,' I tell him. 'Proper evil.'

He laughs. 'It doesn't work, does it, David?' He's trying to hoist himself further up on his pillows. He's wincing, he gasps out with pain.

'What doesn't?'

'All that super power crap.'

I look down. His pyjamas are beige with brown trim. Polyester. He's lying over the sheets and the blankets that they brought with them from Australia.

'They do,' I say. 'They always do. We just have to

believe in them more.'

He shakes his head. 'They didn't do anything for me. I thought I could sort them lads out. I thought I could show them and stop them picking on me for once… just for once, I wanted to show them, in front of my mam and everyone…'

'You did,' I say. 'You showed them. You faced up to them.'

'And got beaten to shit.' He touches the bright bloody bruises on his face. He looks like fruit, like peaches and plums, left in the fruit bowl to rot.

He looks at me. 'It doesn't matter if you face up to them or not. They'll always win. There's more of them. They're… normal. Ordinary.'

In a way I know he's right. I know he didn't show them anything, really.

But I don't want him to feel like this, like it's hope-less.

'Does it still hurt?' I ask him.

'All over,' he says. 'I'm purple all over.'

He sags back and he's given up explaining it all to me. He cries a little bit then, like he can't cover it up any more. His crying tugs his face out of shape.

I'm used to watching people older than me crying. I'm used to sitting and waiting while they finish, wondering whether I should say anything or try to hug them.

'My mam had to put me in the bath,' he tells me. 'She's not done that since I was a little kid. She put me in there with nowt on and she was crying. It was awful.' He clenches his teeth and tries to stop sobbing. 'I won't let her see me like that again.'

I make a decision. 'Let me see you.'

His eyes flash darkly. 'You what?'

'Let me see the bruises. I want to see what they did to you today.'

I want to memorise the bruises like a map. John's different. He's talking to me differently. I want to see him now so I still know it's him.

He shakes his head.

'Come on, John, man. We're mates, aren't we?'

'What good would it do?'

I swallow. 'I want to see.'

'I look like the fucking Elephant Man.'

I smile. 'I don't mind.'

He shakes his head. Then he carefully peels off his

pyjama top. He's skinny as a chicken and bruises are blooming on his chest, arms and ribs. He undoes the cord of his pyjama bottoms and shows me where they were kicking him. His dick's all soft in all the dark, grown-up hair he has. I don't understand how they can still pick on him when his body's grown up like this, like a proper man's.

'You can't look at me like this, you know,' he tells me. 'This would get me, or you, kicked in again. Stuff like this…'

Stuff like what?

'And they think it's weird. They think it's queer. And it isn't right. Boys don't look at each other. They just don't.'

But I'm not listening to him. I'm looking at him, all stretched out and white, bruised purple and black.

'We do,' I tell him. 'We look.'

'Not any more,' he says.

And I can feel a rushing noise in both my ears and I'm starting to use – I know I am – I'm starting to use my super powers for real.

He's got to know. He has to know that they are real.

'What are you doing?'

'It wasn't a lie,' I tell him. 'It wasn't just a daft game. I do have powers.'

'Stop it, David. It's kids' stuff. It's stupid.'

He sounds angry as I put my hands out over him.

Then they start to glow with an unearthly light. It's different to the light from his tissue-papered lamp. It's gentle and white, slowly brightening light. Its comes off both my hands like slow yellow fire and it's reaching out over his whole body. He stares down and he can't move.

'Fuck,' he breathes and his chest rises and falls.

'Sssh,' I tell him, and the radiance increases and slowly and gradually his whole battered, pale body is lit up.

I know it's the last time I'll ever see him like this. Whatever happens, this will scare him. Making it real is going too far. It's too weird even for John. I've gone too far. But it'll prove to him that I wasn't just making stuff up.

'You can't... You can't...'

But I have.

And it's better than I could have imagined. Even I didn't know I could do this.

When the light fades from him and we're left in the soft glow of his lamp, it's plain that every scrap of bruise and cut has gone from his body.

His skin is back to his usual milky paleness. The cuts have sealed up and trapped his blood inside. The deep bruises have rolled away like clouds.

John's back to normal now. We both stare at him. We're both a bit shocked.

He just stares at himself as I get up to go. I feel like I've used up all my powers on him. For now, anyway. It's tired me out. All my strength has gone into him.

But he needed to know.

He gawps at me. 'Just get out,' he whispers. 'Get out of my room.'

I knew he'd be scared. I knew even John wouldn't want it to get this strange.

He's sitting up with nothing on and watching me go. All those comics and posters are around him, chucked just anywhere in his bedroom. He'll believe anything if it's in a film or a comic. But the look on his face just now, it's like he never really wanted the strange stuff to be true.

In their kitchen Maddy is starting on a few days' worth of washing-up.

There's a jam jar filled with dirty paintbrushes. The

water they've been standing in looks like purple tea.

'He wants to sleep,' I tell her.

'Will you come and see him tomorrow?' Maddy asks. 'You know he hasn't got many friends.'

I nod, but I know I won't. I want to, but we won't be friends now. It's gone past that point and I don't know what comes after that. John's older than me. He'll be back in that world of his own.

Maddy looks like she's going to start crying now. All of a sudden I'm wishing people wouldn't talk to me like a grown-up already.

'I suppose I did something wrong,' she says. 'I brought him up wrong, so he hasn't many friends. So he stands out as different. But I don't know, do I? How could I know what the right way is?' She picks up all those unwashed brushes in one hand. 'Ah, listen to me. Spilling out all my cares to you. You're just a kid, David. You don't need to listen to this. To an old woman mithering on. You get yourself on home, pet. It was good of you to come.'

16

We're in the library in Aycliffe town centre. It's a small, square building with too many windows, right by the police station. Mam waits while we look up and down at the stacks. She doesn't like being here, in case our dad is working at the police station and she bumps into him.

The whole place has that disinfectant smell, like school. It won't be long now, till we're back there.

This morning it was cooler again. When we walked down town there were leaves on the path. They go all gingery and dead and you can smell the seasons changing.

When we set off, Brian's sister Kate was standing at her gate and sniffing the air. 'I want to be away before winter comes,' she told Mam.

'Away?' Mam was puzzled.

'Out of here. Out of Aycliffe. Maybe out of England. Des is looking into jobs abroad. Somewhere warmer.'

She chuckled at my mam. Mam was looking surprised and disappointed.

'I thought you were settled here,' Mam said.

Kate shrugs and smiles. 'Hey, we're gypsies. We never settle really. And it's not exactly right for us here. And besides, I can't stay here if my bloody brother's moved in with you, two doors down. Cramping my style.'

Mam smiled.

'It's nearly a new decade,' Kate said. 'Might be time to move on, out of here.'

Mam nodded, but still looked surprised that Kate could decide things like that, just standing by her garden gate and sniffing the air.

'Have you seen Maddy this morning?' Kate laughed.

'Not yet,' Mam said.

'I saw her when she went off to her cleaning job at the church. She was all bright and cheery. I asked her why and she said she'd been up all night, praying for John.'

Mam rolled her eyes.

Kate leaned forward and said, in a lower voice, 'Jeez. She reckons that all of John's bruises and injuries have healed up overnight. She says it's a miracle. And she says that it's all down to her prayers.'

'Never...' Mam murmured.

'That's what she's going round saying.'

I felt sad for a second just then. It was down to me.

It was all down to me, and not to Maddy and her prayers.

'She'll have the lad as crackers as she is,' Mam said. 'Believing in stuff like that.'

'I suppose she needs to believe in something,' Kate said. 'Anyway, John's not come out of his room yet, so no one knows.'

No one is ever going to know. No one but me.

Mam and Kate said goodbye. We turned and walked into town. There were groceries to get. Brian had offered to drive us, but Mam wanted to walk. We left him in the house.

'Do you think Kate will really move away?' I asked Mam as we walked down the burn.

She shrugged and said she didn't know.

'Do you think Maddy's prayers really worked?'

'Don't be daft,' she said. 'It's rubbish. She must be addled. No, he mustn't have been that badly hurt, after all.'

At least I know the truth of it. And I'm glad Maddy has cheered up and is taking all of the credit with her prayers.

That protects my secret identity. No one but John really knows what I can do.

But everything has changed and I know he won't talk to me again.

Chris is borrowing one of my salmon-pink library tickets. His own have been blacklisted because he's had three picture books out for three years and he still can't find them anywhere. He cried when he saw the letter from the library; what they called the official notification of his exclusion: 'Borrower Blacklisted: Withdraw Tickets.' I've been a member of Aycliffe library since I was five and it's only today, because Mam's come in with us, that I'm allowed to go into the fiction section.

It's usually Dad who brings us on Saturday, before we go to the policemen's baths in Durham. He says, 'What do you want to look at the fiction books for? Fiction's for girls, you know. That's what they read.'

'He never said that?' Mam whispers, shocked. She's standing with all our shopping in carrier bags.

'So we're not even allowed over this side of the room,' I say.

'He's an ignorant pig,' says Mam.

Now there's an excitement about being in fiction and choosing just anything off the shelves.

Dad makes us stick to science and history. And I borrow books about dinosaurs and cavemen, astronomy and Roman times. 'General knowledge and science is what you need,' he says. 'You can't go far wrong with that, lads. That's how you find out how the world works.'

For a while I was obsessed with the idea of evolution: with diagrams of the molten cores of worlds; with the ordered seating plans of solar systems. I fell in love with creatures from mythology. I knew which lizardy beings walked the Earth in which sweltering periods of all its prehistory. I knew how Roman legionaries wiped their bums (sponges on a stick) and where they slept when they paraded Hadrian's Wall. I knew all the facts of living in both history and myth. And Chris would be taking out picture books that dad thought suitable, selecting them from the small box in the middle of the floor. He was bored to tears. No wonder he got his own salmon-pink library cards blacklisted.

'Non-fiction!' Mam sighs, when I tell her all of this. 'That's barbaric! I had no idea. Why didn't you say?'

I shrug. I must have thought it was normal and that Dad was just right: that fiction was only for girls.

'He's a bad influence on you,' Mam says. 'Giving you

funny ideas. He'll have you playing football and joining the police force, the army, all sorts.' She sighs and directs us firmly towards the novels and the short stories and lets us have our pick.

'What harm can fiction – just fiction – ever do to a boy?' she asks.

I think this over for a bit while I'm looking at the shelves.

If it does cause harm, then it's already happened. Because I already believe in impossible things.

'Mam,' I ask her, as we stand in the library, 'do you remember telling me that I could do anything? Absolutely anything with my life? And that nothing would be impossible if I wanted it?'

She gives me a funny look. 'When did I say that?'

'When I was born. The first day I was born.'

She laughs and picks up the shopping bags off the waxy library floor.

'If I did, you wouldn't be able to remember it, would you?'

'I think I do. I think I remember hearing your voice.'

'Well...' she says. 'You can. You can decide for yourself what your life will be like. That's the point.'

I've got an armful of books. They're the most interesting books I could find. The ones with the most outlandish things happening in them because that's what I want to read.

I want to believe in powers of all different kinds.

I can't be the only boy like this.

When we get back home we have Heinz tomato soup for dinner and sugary doughnuts from the bakery. Mam puts the *Xanadu* record on again. Then she remembers that today's meant to be the first day of Radio Aycliffe, which is broadcast from up the ramp in the town centre. It's the first time we've had a local radio station and they reckon they're taking requests all day. She finds the right wavelength and Blondie is playing.

'It's all up-to-the-minute New Wave music,' Mam tells us. 'You should like this. Can you believe it's coming from just down the town centre?'

She reckons that, because it's local, it should be easier to get your requests put on. She tells us to think of one and we'll ring up. Chris decides he wants 'Can You Feel the Force?' because he thinks it's about *Star Wars*.

There's a knock at the door then and Mam's

puzzled to see a delivery man in a blue overall with a huge parcel in brown cardboard. We come out to see and he's making her sign his clipboard. 'But what is it?' she asks.

'It's a fridge, love.' He's manoeuvring it into our kitchen.

'But I can't afford a fridge! I haven't ordered a fridge!' She's starting to look worried.

'Hey, don't ask me, love,' he snaps, huffing and puffing with the wrapped up fridge. 'I just do the deliveries.'

Mam's staring at the carboard and the see-through plastic. 'It looks like a good one...' she says.

Then the garden gate is banging open again and Brian's dad is there, with his anorak zipped right up. When he sees what's going on he gives a shout and laughs.

'You sent this?' Mam cries. 'But you can't! I mean...'

Arnold watches the delivery man leaving and he taps the top of the fridge. 'Oh, course I can.' He passes her the cold pint of milk he's brought. 'You can't be without a fridge in all this heat. Here, get that kettle on.'

When we sit having our tea the Police are playing on Radio Aycliffe.

Mam picks up the phone and tells Arnold, 'I'm going to phone up and ask for a record for you. That's how we can thank you for the fridge.'

'Hey, really, there's no need.'

But she's already got the free local paper out and pressing the numbers on the Trimphone. 'Now, what song would you like?' she asks as it rings at the other end. 'It's ringing!'

'Oh, I don't know.' He grins. 'I don't know any songs…'

'Come on!' Mam laughs. 'Think of one!'

His face lights up. 'What about the music from *The Dambusters*?'

Then Mam is talking with someone at the other end, very politely. 'Oh,' she says. 'All right. Well, it's for Arnold. Yes. And it's to say thank you for the new fridge, from Mary, David and Christopher.' She nods. 'Thank you.' And puts she down the phone.

'They say you might not get *The Dambusters*,' she tells Arnold. 'But they'll play you something just as good instead.'

'Good,' he nods and beams. 'Well, I'd better help you fix that fridge up, hadn't I?'

The Trimphone gives one of its sudden, high-pitched rings.

'Oh, maybe they've found your record,' Mam tells him.

'Aye,' he laughs.

Mam picks up the phone but her face darkens and she frowns. You can tell by the way she's standing who it is. And you can hear, even from the little tinny whisper in her ear, that it's Dad's voice.

She looks at us bad-temperedly. 'He wants to talk to one of you two about the weekend. He says he wants to make plans for what you're all going to do.'

She sighs and holds the receiver out. I know it'll be me who'll have to talk with him. I really don't want to. But I'm surprised, then, because Chris has reached over the coffee table and taken the phone off Mam.

'Hello?' he goes, and listens.

Mam's saying to Arnold, 'The bloody bloke knows that he's not supposed to phone here...' She shudders. 'I even hate the sound of his voice...'

We all jump then as Christopher starts yelling into the phone, 'We all hate you, pig-face! We never want to see you... ever again!' Then he smashes the phone down as hard as he can.

Mam runs round the coffee table to get him. 'Chris! What are you doing?' She sounds really cross. He was looking pleased with himself a second ago, but now he doesn't look so sure.

'I was just telling him...' he says.

'This'll cause bother,' Mam groans. 'He'll say I've been brainwashing you again. Now we'll have to phone up and you'll have to talk with your dad, David, and say that Chris was just joking ...'

Oh, great.

Arnold says, 'I don't see why the lad shouldn't say what he wants. If that's what he thinks of his dad, he's right to tell him...'

We sit quiet for a moment, staring at the phone.

Then the Radio Aycliffe DJ comes on loud over the speakers with his fake American accent, telling us he's had a request for an Arnold and it's to thank him for the new fridge.

Arnold claps his palms on his knees and goes, 'Well, you bugger! I'm famous now!'

'Tragedy' by the Bee Gees comes on.

'What the hell's this?' he laughs.

'Tragedy, by the Bee Gees,' Mam says.

'Ha!' he barks. 'That's the story of my bloody life.'

17

This Saturday night, Dad's out with a different woman.

He chucked Rachel midweek because he said she was getting too serious too soon. Now he's met someone who's more fun and he's taken her out clubbing.

There's been a funny atmosphere with him all day. We sat in a burger bar having strawberry milkshakes and Chris was making horrible sucking, gurgling noises with his straw.

'Do you have to?' Dad snapped. He hadn't mentioned how Chris had yelled at him down the Trimphone the other day. I thought he was about to, and to tell Chris off, but he didn't. And he hasn't mentioned all the palaver last Sunday, either. We don't go to the swimming baths and we don't go to the pictures. We sit in the Wimpy and Dad orders burgers and he flicks through the evening paper, frowning.

Wimpy have got an offer on where you get cards of superheroes to stick on a wall chart.

Then he drove us up to South Shields to my Little Nanna's. We went to Ripon's and she bought Chris a cuddly Kermit the frog and me a model kit of Frankenstein's monster. His hands and face are *luminescent*, which means they glow in the dark.

As we watch telly late on Saturday night, Granda is putting the model kit together in the kitchen. It gets so late that we're still sitting there when Dad gets in alone with red eyes.

My Little Nanna glances at him. 'Did you have a nice time, son?' He pulls a face.

I'm still wide awake. I'm sitting on the upended golden pouffe and riding it like a pony by the drinks cabinet and bar. I can balance exactly on the back two castors of the pouffe and it's like I'm practising how to levitate. I'm keeping myself up with an impregnable force shield. It's quite a feat of concentration. I'm a bit bored with *Match of the Day*, which all of the others are glued to. Dad sits with Martin and soon they're shouting at the footballers on the telly, 'Go-waannn, lad! Ha'waaay! Scoooore!'

Christopher must be bored too, because that's when he comes over to me and gives me a firm shove off my velour perch.

I lose my balance and fall backwards against the wall

and bust my head open. I hear the sound of it before I feel it. Inside my head it sounds like someone kicking a football. I've been drop-kicked into *Match of the Day.*

There's a stunned silence for a moment.

I'm lying all crumpled up on the carpet. My ears are ringing. And then it starts to hurt.

The first thing I know is that my Little Nanna has shot over and is rummaging through my bloody hair. It feels like it's just been washed. But there isn't that clean feeling. My whole head feels stickily wet, like I've been covered in oil or hot gravy. It's sliding down over my face and the back of my neck. I'm starting to feel a bit dizzy.

'Stitches! He'll need stitches!'

Dad gulps, going red. 'I'll get the car.'

Granda's come through, holding the half-done model kit of Frankenstein's Monster.

'Eee, lad,' he says, shaking his head and inspecting the damage. 'That wall is the only solid bloody wall in the whole house.'

I can take in the words they're all saying, but it's like a nightmare, like I'm seeing it from miles away. Their faces are coming closer and they're all bulging outwards like when you look at your face in the back of a spoon.

They look angry and scared. I keep thinking I should feel the same.

Christopher has started to wail. He's being ignored and that only makes him worse. Martin carries on spooning broth into his mouth, one eye on the telly, the other on his pools coupon. I get dressed again, clutching my head.

You mend heads with vinegar and brown paper. The vinegar would stink.

They're standing me up in the front room and it's my Little Nanna dressing me in front of everyone, like I'm a little kid again. I should be ashamed, letting them all see me like this, bleeding all over with, for a terrible second, nothing on. Before I know it I'm back in my outdoor clothes and someone's pulling my coat on, like I can't do anything for myself. Now I feel special. Being taken out at night. Like I'm going on a trip in the middle of the night when good kids should really be in bed. They hustle me outside. Then I'm standing by the car, trying to lower myself in. The cold out here is a shock, especially on the hot, wet mess at the back of my head. For the first time I feel like crying. I know I'm going to the hospital and I just want to tell them that it'll be OK. I can just stay

indoors and heal myself. I don't want to go to somewhere like a hospital in the middle of the night. Now I
feel a bit sick. My Little Nanna asks sensibly, 'Do you
want to go to the toilet before you go?' I decide that I
probably do. So I'm swept back indoors again and the
staircase in front of me is wobbling and blurring.

It's just like having a fever, like when you have the flu
really badly.

Everyone's still shouting as they hurry me upstairs.

I meet Martin on the top landing, coming out of the
toilet. He's still chewing. 'You've got blood all down
your face,' he says.

I look in the bathroom mirror, prepared for the
shock. My face has gone all white. I look a bit green. It's
my expression that really makes me feel shocked. It's
seeing my face that makes me realise that something has
really happened and it could be quite serious. I could die!
I could have brain damage! There's a delicious and exciting rush of fear that comes with that thought. This isn't
something I'm making up or imagining. I'm really, really
injured and now I can see the blood – all thick and dark
like the sweetest jam – seeping out from under my hair.
My hair's gone dark like I'm wearing a wig.

I hurry downstairs and feel as if I'm flying, and they're still all looking at me like I'm not even me any more. They rush me out to the car and strap me in the passenger seat. My usual place. But this time Dad can't go into his usual interrogation scene. I'm injured. My brains might be leaking out even now as we drive and I can't be answering his usual questions or listening to him go on. I'm aware of Granda in the back seat, murmuring and giving directions that dad doesn't need. I'm the centre of attention now and I don't have to do anything. I don't have to listen to them at all.

Soon we're tearing through the quiet streets of South Shields. As usual, Dad thinks he's driving a police car.

I feel oddly calm about the whole thing.

I'm counting the yellow double-deckers that are still going about in the night. They're the exact yellow, I realise, of the cheap baked beans that Little Nanna gets from the butchers where they work. Whenever she leaves the shop she takes bagfuls of tins and chops and sausages. They get all their food from the shop. You don't see those baked beans on sale anywhere else. They must be a special kind. But the juice they're in is just the same colour as the double-decker buses in South Shields. This must mean something, because I'm thinking about it all the way to the hospital.

When we get to Casualty, Dad is muttering about Mam and what she's going to say. He's right to worry about that. If Mam was here she'd kill him. And she wouldn't look as scared as he does. She'd put a brave face on for me.

We sit in the waiting room, in school chairs, and Dad keeps looking at my scalp. My hair is all plastered down with blood and that's hiding the real wound. 'She should have got your hair cut.' He braces himself for phoning Mam.

I stare at the cracked lino. The posters to do with car accidents. He comes back from the phone furious. 'There's no answer. She's out again.'

So we sit and wait. I know I've gone very quiet. But the ringing has come back in my ears. I should tell them that I feel OK really, but I don't. I just watch with interest everything that's going on around us and my whole skull feels tight and numb. Dad's counting the minutes. He looks at his watch all the time. He gets up and walks around on the yellow lino. He looks at his watch and he won't really look at me. Half an hour goes past. Then 40 minutes. He's about to go and cause a fuss for us having to wait so long.

When my number gets called out Granda is in a fitter state to help me to the curtained cubicle. He watches as the safe, Scottish nurse hoists me on to the crackling bed. Little Nanna was right. I'm going to get stitches. The fat nurse is threading her needle and smiling and she expains what will happen and what it will feel like. Granda holds my hand as her cold needle goes in once, twice, three times and I feel my skin all over my face tighten in time to her sharp tugging. I feel the slick black twine run through the holes in my swollen skin. I squeeze Granda's hand until his bones click. For a moment I think about Granda's cool, dry skin on his hand and how it's meant to be the same as mine because we're in the same family. But how, even though we're the same and he's holding my hand, he can't feel what I feel in my head, and I can't feel the pressure of my own hand on his, digging in my nails when the needle stings. I feel very separate.

The big nurse gives me a Jelly Tot and then she's gone.

I sit up. Granda pats my shoulder. 'You've been in the

wars, bonny lad.'

I nod and feel a numb weight building up in my head.

'But there wasn't a squeak out of you! Not a peep! Have you heard the noise from the other kids in here?'

I listen. For the first time I can hear the moaning and the whining. The nurse is going round the others and sorting them out, making them well.

It's like turning the sound up on the telly. The whole world is coming flooding back to me.

'Stitches in your head!' Granda smiles. I've never heard him talk so much. 'You never made a sound. Wait till I tell your Nanna. Some, you know, some would scream. Listen!'

I get put to bed in the spare room. Aunty Charlotte's old room, purple and gold, still crammed with candles, carved antelopes and swirly, psychedelic paintings. The large mottled mirror casts a milky sheen over the bed set-tee. Dad is putting Christopher to bed in the next room. When he leaves, I can hear Christopher whimpering to himself so I go through. I'm still a bit dizzy.

'Hey.'

He sits up in the double bed, clutching Kermit. His

eyes are wider than the frog's.

'Does it hurt?'

'No. It was an adventure. It was worth it.'

He brightens up. 'What's Mam going to say?'

'I don't know.'

'I'll blame it on Dad.'

'OK.' I tuck him in again. 'Go to sleep.'

When I go back on to the landing I can hear the worry in their voices downstairs. Nervy cigarettes over one last pot of tea. Fresh smoke comes up the stairs, strange and homely at the same time. Granda is describing again how brave I've been. I go back to my bed settee and lie down, the pillow pulsing beneath my head. I should try to sleep, but I'm reeling with everything that's happened.

Later the door comes open. I can see it in the mirror. There's a bit of light as Martin comes into the room. I watch him loom, his pink and brown body as he undresses.

He rubs his telly-swollen eyes with his fingertips. I listen to the way his joints crack. The slap of the elastic on his pants as he pulls them down.

He's sharing the bed settee with me and lets in the

cold air as he feels between the sheets. His weight sags us down. I hear his breath shallow out as he falls asleep almost straight away. His thick bare arm, his father's watch still on his wrist, resting over the continental quilt. I lie basking in the warmth from his back. Like Granda's, his body is related to mine as well. And I'm thinking about how one day, not long, I'll be bigger too. I'll be lying like this and I'll be too strong to get hurt.

The wasteground at the back of their house is like a pretend countryside. Trains clank by on rails the colour of tea. The Hoover groans downstairs, already at work on last night's mess. The light is yellow, spiking out the pattern on the curtains.

I'm curled right into Martin. His heavy arm tucks me into him, the other making a pillow for my head. His breath whistles coolly on to the wounded patch. My legs lie stickily along his, warmed and comfortable.

He wakes and gets up carefully. His hair is dry as straw.

'How's your head?' he asks. I'm thinking – a moment ago I felt his new stubble against the tender bit of my head.

'Good,' I say.

He dresses, pulling on his jeans, zipping up, snagging himself. 'Granda said you were dead brave.' He smiles.

'Yeah.'

He pulls on his football shirt.

I watch bubbles of grease dancing over the surface of the gravy boat.

'Everything swims in grease,' Mam always says. She used to hate coming here for Sunday lunch.

A plump wodge of beef sits spitting on the table. It's twined in roasted string.

Aunty Charlotte has turned up in a paisley dress with a lacy neck.

She's talking about the challenge of her new job, which is teaching mentally handicapped people how to paint. She used to paint signs for shops. She's smaller than Martin – her own son – and seems to make herself even smaller as they sit together. Her elbows are tucked in and she drums her fingers on the Formica.

The other aunty, Emily, and her postman husband – my godfather, Steven, with the invisible moustache – sit opposite me. His moustache is invisible because it's so fair. The stubble that Martin's getting is thicker than his. Steven is talking to Dad about Sunderland and promotion to the first division. Dad is getting excited about it. Emily chews with her mouth open, smacking her glossy lips and making 'mmm' noises while others talk. My Granda shoots her a look. My Little Nanna carves the roast into untidy bits.

They talk loudly, all the time. There are no quiet corners to the conversation. They brag and sigh over my injury. Chris lowers his head over his plate and won't sit up straight. Then the trifle appears and he begins to cheer up. It's his weekly job to sprinkle it with hundred-and-thousands. I look. They aren't spread very evenly. The family are talking about law and order. Dad is the expert.

'You prig,' snaps Aunty Charlotte, waving her hand. 'Put you in a uniform and suddenly you know it all.'

'Well,' says Emily, 'he's been trained. He ought to know it all. We should be glad of him, keeping us safe in our beds at night.'

'He's still a prig.'

Dad looks annoyed. 'Charlotte is an anarchist.'

My Little Nanna gives them both a sharp glance. 'No, she isn't.'

Charlotte sighs. 'I might be.'

'Look,' Dad begins, 'you don't see enough of the world. There's more to life than painting pretty pictures...'

'You patronising bugger!'

'There are some really nasty people out there...'

'Oh, tell me about it!'

Little Nanna pitches in. 'Just last week he told you about that man who was kidnapping bairns in Ferryhill.'

'You see –' Dad stares past the lemon-coloured venetian blinds for inspiration – 'there's a good side and a bad side. Right and wrong. I'm with the white side, that's how I see it, automatically on the good side. It's as simple as that... and everyone else... who isn't... is... ehm... black.'

Charlotte laughs in his face. 'Racist as well!'

'What about minor offences?'

This is Steven. He speaks more quietly, not being a blood relation.

They all look at him.

'Minor offences?' asks my Little Nanna sharply.

'Do you,' Steven mumbles, 'do you see them the same as kidnapping and murder and rape and that? I mean, in the eyes of the law?'

Dad settles back. 'It depends.'

'Minor *infringements*,' Aunty Charlotte says, jabbing her spoon. I look at her and wonder what she might have been up to. I look at Steven and he seems really worried. Little Nanna is looking at him too. 'That's what they're called,' Aunty Charlotte says. 'There's all sorts of little ways of doing wrong. You might not even know you're doing it, but you're outside the law. And there's always the police waiting there, to see when you step out of line.'

'You see,' says Dad, 'little things add up.'

My Little Nanna nods and goes round doling out the last of the Bird's Trifle. The jelly spoons out with sharp sucking noises. I feel heavy and hemmed in.

'It's the same as anything,' Little Nanna says. 'Every little thing counts.' She grins, charm bracelets clinking.

I wonder if I've ever made a minor infringement.

'You let them by, one by one and what do you end up with?' Dad looks serious. 'Chaos.'

'Anarchy,' says Emily.

'Looting,' says Steven gloomily.

Charlotte rolls her eyes. 'You're not telling me that

you've never broken the law yourself. Even in minor ways. Speeding or taping record albums or disturbing the peace when you've had a few pints?'

Emily says, 'What about weeing in the street?'

Everyone looks at her.

'What?'

'That's a civic disturbance, isn't it? What about you, a copper... what if you got caught short in the street and you couldn't find a toilet?'

'This is ridiculous,' groans Charlotte. 'It's like arguing with children.' She leaves the table.

'Would you pull your pants down in the street and do your business there, even if it was an offence?'

Christopher and Martin start to giggle.

'Emily,' Granda begins.

'Yes?'

'Keep your mouth shut when you're eating, pet.'

Dad says, 'If you live a normal, decent life, like ordinary people do, then you've got nothing to worry about. That's the point. You just have to keep your head down and be the same as everyone else. If you fit in, then you've really got nothing to worry about.'

Charlotte glares at him from the doorway. 'Well, that

just sounds like hell.'

'I forgot.' Dad laughs. 'She's an artist, isn't she?' And he pulls a face to make the others laugh. 'She always thought she was different. Special. Well, that doesn't get you anywhere. That just makes life difficult. For you and everyone else.'

Charlotte is leaving the room and I want her to stay. I want her to explain it to me. But she's gone off.

My Little Nanna starts siding the dishes up. 'You're all special to me, you lot.'

Dad shrugs. He's got his mouth full, too, as he talks, but Granda doesn't tell him off. 'Special to you, Mam, aye. But not in the eyes of the world. Out there, we're just ordinary. And everyone has to fit in. That's the way the world works. I know.'

After dinner the family play darts in the outhouse, which they call a lobby.

It's green and smells of coats. I stand at the bottom of the garden, watching over the wasteground at the back of the rail tracks. I can hear their shouting and cheering indoors.

I'm standing on a pile of gingery compost shunted

against the iron fence. It's crumbly under my good, weekend shoes. It's a cooler day. The twigs and weeds of the garden are dry and crackling. I turn to see my Little Nanna picking her way through the garden towards me, her best darts in her hand. She calls them her arrows. Her lucky arrows, with Union Jacks on their plastic flights.

'I've brought them out with me, so none of them buggers can nick them.'

She heaves herself up on the compost heap beside me. 'I've come out to see to see my favourite grandson.'

'You say you don't keep favourites.'

'I've got three favourites!' she laughs, plucking at the plastic feathers of the darts. 'I won these at the club. You could play today, if you wanted.'

'I'm not very good.'

'You don't have to win.'

There's a lull. We listen to the yells from the lobby, the cries of 'Cheat!' The family's usual babble.

A pillar of smoke goes up from the crematorium over the wasteground.

'There goes another poor bugger,' my Little Nanna says.

'Everyone in this family always has to win,' I say.

There's a pause. I could bite my own tongue off.

'It's nice to win,' she says. Then I wait for her to add the usual thing, the thing they always say at school, about being a good loser too.

But that never comes. That's it: it's nice to win.

'Different people like different things, David.'

'I know.'

'We're a family. Quite a close and boisterous one. And most of us like the same things. Football, darts, good grub and arguing with each other in a friendly sort of way. You don't like those sort of things, do you?'

'Not really.' I touch the wound on my head and it feels sticky again. 'I don't like arguing.'

'Why not? It's harmless... just talking, really. But loud.'

'Mam and Dad argued.'

She sighs.

'Who won there, Nanna? Who won the divorce?'

'No one wins those, pet.'

'Dad thinks they do. He thinks he won. He's on the white side.'

'It doesn't count for things like that.'

'Dad has to win, doesn't he? Else he cries.'

'He's a man. Men are mostly big bairns. You'll find that out.'

We look at the line of trees at the far end of the waste-ground. When I was smaller I thought it was a jungle, stuffed with birds of paradise, tapirs, glittering snakes. My Little Nanna egged me on with my imagining.

Now I know that it's just the trees around the crematorium.

My Little Nanna says, 'When you come here for the weekend, do you miss your mam?'

'I worry about her being by herself. She has us in the week and she's busy. Then it's the weekend and she's alone.' I'm lying. I'm lying to my Little Nanna. But it wouldn't do to tell her that Mam has Brian at home now. That would open a whole other can of worms. Little Nanna hasn't even met Brian. She doesn't know who he is because they're in separate dismensions from each other. I'm only lying to her because it'll keep things simpler that way. Grown-ups like things to be simpler. And anyway, it was true for a long time. Mam did sit quietly alone while we were away at weekends. She was left by herself every week and that worried me.

I go on: 'It's like... Dad has us then and he tries to enjoy himself and sweep us along in it.' I look at my Little Nanna. 'We like to see you, Nanna. But it looks like Dad's won. He's got everyone looking after him. We're all wanting him to have a nice time.'

Her face has gone hard. 'He's my son.'

She shrugs and starts to climb down off the compost pile.

Later on they're all gathered in the living room watching Martin do press-ups for money. Aunty Charlotte sits stiffly on the chesterfield settee, smoking fiercely and watching. Martin's doing his exercises one-armed, the other crooked up his back. My Little Nanna is counting from her armchair, clapping each time his nose brushes the carpet, adding another ten pence to the stack she's building on the arm of her chair. Granda stands proudly, one eye on the glittering stack. Chris is sitting by Aunty Charlotte, content.

On my way upstairs to check my head I find Dad sitting on the stair carpet, talking into the phone. 'Of course it isn't serious. No, it couldn't have been.' He looks up and his eyes are bloodshot.

'Come here,' he puts one hand over the telephone. 'Tell your mother that you're all right.'

I take the receiver.

'David? What's been happening?' She sounds shrill. The calm of her weekend has been ruined. I explain the accident.

And suddenly I know that I don't want to be here. I want to be at home, in Aycliffe, with her.

She asks, 'Was he neglecting you?'

Dad's brow furrows as he listens in.

'I should have known,' Mam says. 'All them lot in that place. Like a madhouse. You could fall out of a window and they'd never notice. Christopher's all right, isn't he?'

'He's fine.' Then I forget myself. 'He's bored, but ok.'

Dad's stare hardens.

'I want him to bring you both home now.'

'We're not due back till tonight...'

'Put him back on. I'm going to tell him.'

As I hand him the phone I feel relieved. We can be home inside the next hour if he gives in. Free of awkward scenes and the threat of offending someone. Dad puts on a sneering voice.

'The court decided I get all of Sunday as well.'

I can just about hear Mam's tinny reply. That it's up to me and Chris, what we want to do.

'They want to stay here. They're with their family. Their blood family.' He looks at me. 'You want to stay here, don't you?'

I turn and hurry up the stairs. It's Make-Your-Mind-Up-Time again. Like that day with Mam sitting curled into her armchair: 'I've asked your dad to leave.'

He was crying.

'Oh, go on, Mam,' I say. 'Let him stay.'

She shakes her head quickly. 'No,' she says.

I realise he's got his hands on my shoulders, squeezing them too tight as she talks.

'He can't,' she says. 'He's got to go.'

'Right,' he says, with his teeth clenched together.

In the bathroom I rub a little warm water into my scalp. The water in the basin turns pink.

I'm looking into the mirror and I'm staring into my own eyes.

I'll give up everything. I'll renounce all my super powers and everything, and I'll go back to being a normal, ordinary human boy if only. I close my eyes, concentrating on my vow... if only we can have a more normal life. If only we don't get dragged about all over the place any more.

More than ever, right now, I want to go home.

I want life to be simpler than any of this.

I hear Dad slamming the phone down hard.

I go downstairs.

In the living room Martin has crawled exhaustedly to sit by his mam, counting his ten pences. Dad is announcing to everyone, 'She wants them back right now.'

My Little Nanna swivels around in her armchair like Davros. 'She can't have them.'

Christopher's eyes widen at this.

'She blamed us for neglecting them.'

'It was an accident...' Granda begins.

'It was just kids playing,' Little Nanna says. 'Bound to happen. Christopher didn't know what he was doing.'

Christopher solemnly bursts into tears.

'Look what she's caused now.'

'She's broken up our family Sunday,' my Little Nanna says. 'She's vindictive.'

I'm turning red. I can feel a surprising trickle and burn in my own eyes.

'Now they're both at it.'

Aunty Emily is mashing chocolate biscuits in her open mouth and she grasps me with both arms, tousling my hair, which hurts. Across the room Martin opens a bag of crisps and looks bored with us all.

My Little Nanna clasps her knees with both hands and I watch her charm bracelets slide down to her wrists. 'That's it, then.' She looks from Granda to Dad. 'This is it. She's won. They'll have to go back.'

Chris, confused, starts to wail.

Dad says, 'David reckons they're both bored here, anyway.'

My Little Nanna sounds choked. 'Bored?' She eyes me. 'Do you ever want to come back, David? Do you ever want to see us again? Are you that bored?'

I feel the oily trickle of blood down my neck, on to my t-shirt. Not oil. Gravy, with the bubbles of grease in it from the Sunday lunch. It's leaking out of my head.

Chris is moaning, 'I hate it, I hate it.' He thinks Dad is going to arrest him, for the minor infringement of breaking open my head.

I notice that Little Nanna's black wig is askance. She says slowly, 'I think it's for the best if they don't come again. At least…' She cuts through dad's bark of dismay. 'At least for a while. It's too much for them. They're too excitable. She's got them highly-strung. Like she is.'

Dad nods. This is the last word.

Halfway down the A1 he asks, 'And me? Do you want to see me again?'

Chris is in the back seat as usual and he keeps quiet. He wants me to answer for both of us.

'I'm still your flesh and blood. I'm still your dad, aren't I?'

I look at his red and swollen face, the slumped fleshiness of him as he drives. He takes one hand off the wheel and puts it round my shoulders. I can feel the blood on my neck slicking and sticking itself on his wrist.

I stare out of the passenger window at the industrial estates and the lines of dark houses. Each street-light represents a family of four, maybe.

I lean forward so I won't bleed on his new seat covers.

18

'She won't even let me come to the house,' he says. He's fixed his eyes on the motorway. He won't look at me.

After last weekend, when he caused such a fuss in the street because he reckoned she was late back to meet us, I'm not surprised, but I don't tell him this. It's just as well. He'd only be shouting outside our house again, shouting in Mam's face, shouting her down.

He can't go to the house now because Brian's there. Brian doesn't want him anywhere near. Brian gets a say-so, now that he's moved in with us. It's like Brian's laying down the law, only doing it through Mam. If Dad did come to the house, I wonder if Brian would come out of the kitchen to stop Dad shouting. Maybe they'd roll around in the grass and they'd be hitting each other.

'We've got to meet them in Durham,' Dad says.

Mam gave him the instructions on the phone at my Nanna's. He didn't look pleased. We sat in silence after my Little Nanna told him that we had to go back. They all looked at us like we'd done something terrible. They didn't say anything else to us until Dad had made the plans with Mam.

It was kind of like that point in the story when everyone's mask drops off and you see the real faces underneath. Those faces didn't look very pleased with us. It was awful sitting there. Chris edged closer to me along the settee.

Little Nanna and Granda didn't come out to wave at us when we drove away. They never did their usual thing of standing in their front doorway till we were out of sight. They sat where they were and then we went.

Our meeting place this afternoon in Durham is the halfway point between South Shields and Aycliffe. Dad has his instructions and he couldn't argue with them or Mam because, as she told him, he was in the wrong. He'd let me get hurt. He hadn't been responsible.

He feels guilty, but he can't do anything about it. He's given in to everyone, his mam, my mam, and he hates it.

He drives into the centre of the old, empty town. And he pulls up on the town side of Old Elvet Bridge. The stone of the bridge and all the buildings is worn away, black and brown. There's no one here on a Sunday afternoon. It's like some disaster's taken place.

'What's going on?' Chris pushes forward to ask me.

'Wait,' Dad says.

Below us the water is sluggish. The oldest, darkest water in all of England. Above the bridge there's the castle and cathedral looming right over us. It makes you feel tiny, sitting here in the car with no one about. Then I start thinking about the green river underneath and wondering how deep the water goes. I start feeling dizzy again. It's like my mental super powers have gone crazy all at once. The telepathy and telekinesis secretly at my disposal have starting buzzing and going mad in my head, all concentrated around the stitches in my skull, like they're bursting to get out. Snapping the twine of the stitches.

But my powers are ebbing away. I've forsworn them. It's like I said. I'll stop having the magic powers if things can just be more ordinary. For a moment back there at my Little Nanna's, that's what I thought I wanted. To be just the same as everyone else and with no complications going on.

We're sitting in the car and I'm waiting in the silence with this buzzing in my head. And I can't think of anything worse than being just ordinary. What if I've bled all my powers out, all over the North-East, through that wound in my head? What if my blood never runs fast through me again? What if I never feel it doing that pounding and all that mysterious whizzing through my body ever again? I don't want that. I want to keep on being me.

It's all 'What Ifs'. It's a 'What If universe. That's where we are.

Then, exactly on the hour, Mam comes walking over the bridge in her long coat.

She's by herself, walking along at her own pace like she just happens to be there. I know she's watching for us. She's squinting and staring ahead, to make sure he's brought us where he's supposed to.

It looks wrong, Mam standing just by herself.

She stands in the middle, right in the middle.

'OK...' Dad says. 'There she is.'

'What's she doing standing there?' Chris says.

'She's waiting for you,' Dad says. 'For you two. She won't come any closer. You have to go out to her.'

'What?'

'That Brian is parked over the other side of the

bridge, up by the market square. You two have to walk across and meet her and she'll walk you over there away from me and then Brian will take you back home.'

'This is so weird,' Chris says.

We get ready to get out of the car. We gather up our stuff and Dad's got his eyes on the middle of the bridge, where Mam stands waiting in the late afternoon sun in her long coat.

Dad says to us, 'Kiss your dad goodbye. Come on, lads. Say goodbye. I don't think you'll ever see him again.'

We do as we're told.

We're good kids. So we do as we're told.

Then we get out of his car.

I have to say something else to him. This is the end of something, so you have to have something to say. We're going back into our everyday life. We've made a decision at some point, I'm not even sure when.

'You know,' I tell him, as we shoulder our bags and get ready to walk across. 'Sometimes you grown-ups are just… like, weird. Most of the time… you carry on like mad people.'

He just looks at me.

He looks at me like I'm the one who's strange.

If this really was a comic and it really was the end of a story, there'd be one of those 'Next Issue' boxes, giving me a preview of what's to come. It would give me an idea of the magic, excitement and the new adventures to come. But there's nothing like that. There's just us, standing on a bridge over the river.

Then I close the car door and he watches us, without another word, as Chris and I set off, walking over the old bridge, towards Mam.

Strange Boy's 1970s Glossary

Advocaat

Sickly sweet, bright yellow alcoholic drink also known as eggnog. With lemonade and ice it's a Snowball, which is the kind of drink that, if you were well behaved on New Year's Eve, you might get a little taste of. And then you'd go, 'That's horrible,' and not be able to finish.

All Creatures Great and Small

Mam and Brian always called this 'The Vets'. It was a TV programme about looking after animals in Yorkshire during the war.

Annuals

A book that comes out at Christmas based on your favourite TV show or comic. After Christmas they sold them half price in Stevens the newsagents down town. You always got the Beano Annual and Doctor Who – they were definites. The rest changed each year.

Basil Brush

Argumentative fox on Saturday night kids' TV. He wore a dark green coat and behaved extremely badly towards his co-presenter, of which he had a few. Mam always called this succession of young men Basil's 'dads'. But we knew they weren't really his 'dads'. He was a fox. He used to laugh at his own terrible jokes and go, 'Ha-ha ha ha… boom, boom!' He used to be on the telly right before *The Generation Game* and *Doctor Who*. Saturday nights used to be great.

Battlestar Galactica

It's a bit like *Star Trek*, only better. We went to the pictures to see the film with Dad. These insect fellas were eating all the women in a big beehive and the Cylons were a cross between the Cybermen off *Doctor Who* and the Stormtroopers out of *Star Wars*. Then it was on the telly and it was rubbish. But the book was good.

The Bee Gees

Hairy freaks who sang disco songs, looked terrible and were supposed to be related to each other. Mam and Brian loved them. They did 'Saturday Night Fever' and 'Tragedy'.

Bird's Eye Mousse

Fantastic frozen desserts that came in little tubs. Often with a ripple effect. You got a headache if you ate them too fast.

Charlie's Angels

Bizarre adventure series about three women sent on dangerous missions by a man who lives in a box. I never, ever understood what was going on.

Crossroads

Brilliant drama on ITV every night about a motel somewhere down south run by this woman, Meg Mortimer,
who had a ginger meringue for hair and big glasses. At
the end of the 1970s she left the show, burned down the
motel, faked her own death and ran off on the QE2. It
was rubbish after Meg left.

Dalek City

Where the hideous mechanical Daleks off *Doctor Who*
live. They have sensor pads for opening automatic sliding
doors.

Dallas

One of our favourite shows. About people in America
who all lived in a big house in loads of fields full of cows,
had a swimming pool and who Slept With Each Other.

Damien from The Omen

Very scary child in very scary film from the 1970s. Later
went on to be president of the United States, or something.

Davros

The fella who created the Daleks. He was half a Dalek
himself and probably the scariest thing I had ever seen in
my life.

Disneyland and Disneyworld
The two places that we would have been taken, if anyone
in our family had ever won the Pools (see The Pools) It's
like, a whole country in America where Mickey Mouse
and that lot are real.

Doctor Who
Saturday night TV series in which Tom Baker strode
about laughing in the faces of monsters and villains, all
over time and space. I could vaguely remember a different Doctor, when I was tiny. Mam always said that the
first one – some old fella, when she'd been little – was the
best. It used to be really frightening back then.

The Eagles
Horrible American rock group. The worst kind of whiny
guitars and groaning, wistful singing by men old enough
to know better and too old to wear tight jeans.

The Elephant Man
Bloke who was supposed to look like an elephant.

ELO
Horrible 1970s group with loads of hair who thought
they were the Beatles. They had a spaceship, according to
the sleeve of their most famous record, and went about
playing their music in space.

Emmerdale Farm
ITV midweek drama about farmers. Mam had watched it
from the beginning, so we had to watch as well, though
no one really liked it. Now they just call it *Emmerdale*

Etch-a-Sketch
Brilliant game thing. You had a red board with two dials
and a grey screen full of sand, which you drew on by
twisting the dials. When you wanted to change the drawing, you simply shook it clean and started again. It was
like magic. Eventually Chris stood on mine and smashed
it and it got pushed under his bed for ages so I wouldn't
find out. Other great drawing games of the time includ-
ed Rotodraws and Spirographs.

The Fantastic Four
In Marvel comics, four people were hit by cosmic rays
and developed powers that made them: stretchy (Mr
Fantastic), strong and orange (The Ever-Lovin' Thing),
fiery (The Human Torch) and invisible (The Invisible
Girl).

Fine Fare
Great big supermarket where you could buy anything.
On the adverts there used to be this cartoon family and
this gigantic purse called Purse, who lived with them. I
never understood that.

Fist Fighters
Excellent dolls for boys. If you twisted this thing in their back, their arms moved about so they could punch each other. We had Spiderman, Captain America, and some of the fellas off *Star Trek*.

Flash Gordon
Ancient black and white serial, a bit like *Star Wars* but in half-hour episodes. Flash was always killed at the end of each episode by skiing over a mountainside or being shot by robots, but he was always alive the next episode – even if you had seen him really die.

Ford Capri
A type of 1970s car, often yellow. People drove around in them thinking they were in *Starsky and Hutch* (see: *Starsky and Hutch*).

Geoff Love and his Orchestra
Did two brilliant LPs of superhero and sci-fi themes. They were an orchestra but everything came out a bit like disco. Their versions of *Doctor Who* and *Space: 1999* are superb.

The Green Goblin
Enemy of Spider-man who turned out to be the father of his best friend and insane! Other good Spider-man

villains include Doctor Octopus (who spitefully married Spider-man's Aunt May and had eight arms!) and the Vulture.

Jaws
Very famous film about a man-eating shark. There used to be a great comic strip spoof of it called *Gums*, about a shark with false teeth, in *Whizzer and Chips*, which also featured *The Leopard of Lime Street*. This was about a boy in a northern town who is scratched by a radioactive leopard during a school trip to a zoo. He makes a superhero outfit out of an old leopardskin coat of his mam's, and keeps all his superhero paraphernalia in one of her old handbags and then walks around the streets of Bolton at night, looking for crime spots.

Jeff Wayne's War of the Worlds
Brilliant, terrifying record about Martians invading the world and singing songs about it. Everyone had it. Very expensive.

Legoland
A whole country made out of Lego. Miniature. We never went, but then, we were never really that into Lego. We were certainly never into Mecchano. That was for freaks.

Marvel Comics
American ones were small, in colour and featured only one story, with loads of adverts. They cost 15p and you really had to hunt around in newsagents to find them. British ones cost 10p, were black and white and had many more, shorter stories in, reprinted from the American versions. British titles changed over the years, so that, for example, *Dracula Lives!* and *The Mighty World of Marvel Featuring The Incredible Hulk* both joined up with *The Spectacular Spiderman, The Titans* and *The Planet of the Apes* to make one single comic eventually.

'Mull of Kintyre' by Wings
A single that was number one at the end of the 1970s for about a hundred years. Even though Mam didn't think Paul McCartney was as good as he'd been in the Beatles, she still played this all the time. It was a song about being so rich you can afford to buy part of Scotland and what fun it is living there. Wings used to appear on *Top of the Pops* in a fake Scottish glen, sitting on fake rocks and tussocks of heather, with a whole load of blokes playing bagpipes behind them.

Noddy
Very strange series of books by Enid Blyton, about a doll who lives in a town populated by toys, who runs a minicab firm. He's mostly well-behaved but occasionally goes

into one and causes bother. See titles such as: *You Funny Little Noddy* and *Noddy Pisses Everyone Off On Purpose*.

The Omen
Very scary film about an evil child from the early 1970s. We weren't allowed to watch stuff like that, but John was.

Opal Fruits
Chewy sweets 'made to make your mouth water', now known as Starbursts. The strawberry flavour ones could make you sick (especially on car journeys). The minty versions were called Pacers.

Origin Story
All superheroes have one. The tale – often told in flash-back – of how they gained their mysterious powers, took up a secret identity and pledged to fight evil wherever they found it. The She-Hulk, for example, received an emergency green blood transfusion from her cousin, Bruce Banner, who happened to be the Incredible Hulk.

Pinky and Perky
Kids TV show about two pigs with high-pitched voices. I don't remember the TV show, but I had a record of them singing Christmas Carols. One of the butcher's boys from my grandparents' shop bought it for me as a present when I was born. We used to play it on the morn-

ing of the first day of the Christmas holidays every single year. That was the ritual. It always marked the very beginning of Christmas and was almost unbearably exciting. It began: 'Hey, Pinky. Do you know what day it is?' 'Of course I do, Perky. It's Christmas Eve!' And there's sleigh bells in the background as they start singing *Santa Claus is Coming to Town*. You could tell, really, that the pigs' voices were just, like, ordinary blokes' voices only speeded up.

Planet of the Apes

We saw all the films and the cartoon. Someone had a lunchbox with them on. You could get Fist Fighters of some of the apes. It was about going into the future – to a time (as the Marvel comic put it) 'Where man once stood supreme – Now rules... the Ape!' There was a new film out about it in 2001.

Playschool

A BBC kid's programme for very young children. Mostly in an empty studio, with three presenters pretending to have a great time with the five toys (Big Ted, Little Ted, Humpty, Jemima and Hamble), looking out of windows and singing songs. Like many BBC shows, it was educational. Not to be confused with the similar *Playaway*, which didn't care if it was educational or not, had no toys, more songs and the same presenters.

The Pools

A weekly competition where, if you guessed the scores in a whole load of football games on a Saturday, they'd give you lots of money. A bit like the National Lottery, but more complicated and people got more excited about it.

Pot Noodles

You can still get these. But you've got no idea how exciting they were when they first came out. Like oven chips and instant mash, they were like, really fast food, and that made them impossibly exotic. We once took 24 Pot Noodles with us on holiday to the Lake District. We managed one night's worth and then had to go out for fish and chips and stuff instead. We brought 20 Pot Noodles back with us.

The Rescuers

Disney cartoon about mice who rescue a kidnapped girl with their help of their friends, a dragonfly and an albatross. I could draw all of the characters off by heart.

Revels

Chocolates you can still get where you never really knew what the next flavour was going to be, or whether it would be soft or hard. The coffee ones could make you sick, especially on car journeys.

Shirley Bassey
Singer who's been around for ever who wears wigs and extravagant outfits and waves her arms about when she sings. One of the most famous people in the world.

Spangles
Sucky sweets that came in fruit flavours, but nicer than Opal Fruits. If you sucked them rather than crunching them straight away, you could make the middle disappear first.

Spider-man
Teenage boy who was bitten by a radioactive spider. Fought the Green Goblin, who threw his girlfriend Gwen into the Hudson river and killed her. Great Spider-man things to say include, 'Spider sense, tingling...' and 'It's your friendly neighbourhood Spider-man!'

Star Trek
The old one, where the fellas used to fight more and wear velveteen outfits too small for them. There was this picture during the music at the end of a green woman dancing. We never saw the episode where that happened.

Starsky and Hutch
A show about two American policemen who have a red car with a white stripe down it. It was on very late, so we

were lucky if we got to see it. The double episode about voodoo island was the scariest thing we had ever seen.

Star Wars

The old one, with Darth Vader and all the monsters in the pub and the robots and the fantastic comic. And the figures, which cost 99p each. We had all the toys, except the Death Star playset, which Dad promised to buy for one Christmas, between us. He didn't though and said: 'Well, I looked at it lads, and it was rubbish. It was just a load of cardboard. So I thought we'd make one instead.' We did and it covered the whole floor of one room in his new flat. When we went back the next week, he'd chucked it all out.

Sticker Albums

You'd buy packets of ten stickers, sometimes with chewing gum in, and a book to stick them in. You'd get things like football, or *Star Wars*, or whatever the latest Disney film was, like *The Rescuers*. You'd get doublers and swap them at school. You'd go through your pile of doublers really fast and somebody would be shouting out: 'Got, got, got, need, need, got, need, got.' The sticky stuff they used smelled great. There was a more educational version – the cards given away in boxes of tea, which were about Fantastic Creatures or Space. You had to send off for those books from the tea company. The cards always smelled of tea bags. They were the kind of thing your nanna would collect for you.

2000ad
British sci-fi comic that was too frightening for me to even open.

White Horses
A kids' TV show they used to show in the mornings during the holidays. It was originally in Spanish, but they dubbed it, so that nobody's mouth moved in time to the words.

Why Don't You...?
Another kids' TV show from holiday mornings. Kids from Northern Ireland lived in a huge den and gave you ideas for how to fill up the days. It was always stuff like making cakes or flying kites. We watched it, but we never, ever did anything that they suggested.

The Wicker Man
Very scary film about witchcraft from the early 1970s.

Xanadu
We never saw the film because it looked rubbish. But the song was by Olivia Newton-John, who'd been in *Grease*, which we all loved.

Girl in the Attic

August 2002

Thirteen-year-old Nathan is furious when Mum hauls him
off to Cornwall for Christmas and then tells him they are
to move there for good.

He wants to be back with Dad, with his best friend, Tom,
with his London life.

But then he finds a cottage – and a girl. The girl in the attic.

Who is she, and what is the family secret that haunts her
life? Valerie Mendes' gripping, fast-moving novel explores
the whirlpools of change in teenagers' lives, the strengths
of friendship, and the inescapable, binding pull of love.

ISBN 0 689 83680 5

The Raging Quiet

The Raging Quiet is a haunting and compelling story about the power and determination to overcome prejudice and injustice in a world of witchcraft, feudalism and intolerance.

Set in Medieval times, it tells the story of Marnie and Raver each set apart from the community around them: Marnie because she is a newcomer having been brought to the seaside village by her new - and much older - husband; and Raver because he is the village lunatic.

The Raging Quiet - though embedded in a historical setting - has undiminished relevance today; Marnie and Raver are singled out because they are different.

ISBN 0 689 82706 7

Young Nick's Head

THE YEAR IS 1768, Nicholas Young's mind is made up. He's had enough! Enough of the cruel butcher to whom he is apprenticed and enough of his indifferent father lurking somewhere in the background of his existence. He's had enough of the squalor of his life in London. He is going to run away.

But when he's stowed away on board a small ship he has no idea how famous this journey will be, one of the most famous journeys of discovery in maritime history. Three years it will take before he'll come back to London, three long years of adventure and hardship: an eleven-year-old boy among eighty tough-minded, seafaring men and under constant scrutiny from the gentlemen on board. There's midshipman Bootie who makes every day a living hell for Nick and John Ravenhill the drunken sail maker. But Dr Monkhouse, the surgeon, and Mr Banks, the botanist, stand up for their keen and gifted assistant and one by one Nick befriends the crew.

ISBN 0 689 83508 6

Raspberries on the Yangtze

The Yangtze in this story is not China's biggest waterway, but a rather magical place on the outskirts of a small town in the backwoods of Quebec, Canada.

Nancy, who tells the story, is down-to-earth, practical and dead keen to know everything. Her main challenge in life is her elder brother Andrew. Nancy calls him a 'big thinker'. Their mother calls Andrew a 'dreamer'.

With a few quick brush strokes Karen Wallace transports the reader to a time and a place where children enjoyed a freedom that is impossible to imagine today. The plot moves along quickly, its profound observations and simple truths skilfully unveiled through vivid and authentic dialogue. It's the story of a summer when old dreams are shattered and new dreams are born. For Nancy and her friends, things will never be the same.

ISBN 0 689 82796 2

For Maritsa, With Love

Young Maritsa ignores the angry voices, the insults and the threats. She's heard it all before, and worse. Begging is what she does, and she's good at her job. She knows just how to appeal to the rich commuters of the Paris Metro, how to soften their hearts with her forlorn face and her crumpled tragic note. But somehow, Maritsa knows it's not forever. She catches a glance of a different world and starts dreaming of a career in the movies: pretty dresses and trinkets, fine house and parties...

Turning her back on the gypsy family she lives with and striking out on her own, Maritsa meets that man in the dark glasses and his pretty wife again. They've promised her a screen test. Maritsa will go home famous – at least, that's what she thinks. But soon young, vulnerable Maritsa is being drawn into a dark and seedy underworld, to somewhere nobody should ever have to go.

ISBN 0 689 83636 8